Mage at Midnight

by

Carolyn Brown Heinz

ISBN: 1466468920
ISBN 13: 9781466468924

Table of Contents

Prologue

Late in the fifteenth century, a black goddess slowly emerged from a sculptor's chisel. Chip by chip, her maker released her from the stone, first one delicate arm, then another, and another, until four arms were freed into life. When he came to her face, he uncovered the sweet, intense face of his imagination, the mother of his earliest memories, with wide eyes and an open mouth from which her tongue sensuously protruded. He gave her round breasts that any man would like to touch, a tiny waist any woman would envy, and broad hips from which the world could be born. Her legs were slender and bent from dancing, and beneath her feet, lying prone, the inert body of a man, her spouse, vaguely detailed, barely identifiable except by those who know.

The carver devoted months to bringing the goddess of his imagination into being. He spent many months more, caressing her with his cloths and buffing stones, until she glistened and shone. He spent his days with her under his shed, and at night went to his wife, whose soft body invited him to ecstatic completion of his dreams.

One day Brahmins came to his workshop, three of them, in their white dhotis and sacred threads, to inspect his work. They walked around the black goddess, admiring her delicate hands, her sweet face, her seductive pose. They smiled. The sculptor had captured the essence of their dreams, too. He had fulfilled the longings captured in their books, in their oldest stories, and in their drug-enhanced visions of divinity.

They took her away, hiring a bullock cart to carry her across forests, rivers, and hills to their temple at the crown of a hill overlooking a great river. They enshrined her there with rituals that opened her eyes and established her authority, they thought, for all time.

From there, the goddess who had already enchanted her sculptor and delighted the Brahmins, began her long interaction with the human world.

A century later, from her temple high on the hill, the black goddess felt an evil shadow moving from the west and the south toward her realm. Warriors, bent on destroying temples and the deities who resided in them, moved across the land. With their broadswords they toppled the gods from their pedestals, severing arms, decapitating heads, battering shut the eyes that relentlessly watched them from the earth. She spoke to the Brahmins who served her about the danger to come. Listening, and watching the roads from the west, the Brahmins debated what to do. They were not warriors. How would they protect her?

'Act! Act!' she urged them.

One day, at last, they arrived to worship her as they did every morning, and apologized for what they were going to do. They washed her, then wrapped her body with bolts of cloth, first with scarlet silk, then with white cotton. They lifted her from her dais and laid her on her back on the stone floor. They built a crate and filled it with straw. They gently laid her in, wrapped her in more straw, and nailed shut the lid. Workers were brought to lift the crate onto a bullock cart, which then lumbered out of the city and into the countryside, to the ancestral village of the chief Brahmin.

The crate was set on a platform of stones near the household of the Brahmin family, and bricked over until all that was visible was what seemed to be the foundation of a small storage house. Here the family maintained a constant mound of straw for their cows, who contently munched through dozens of their generations, while the black goddess slept within until the great danger was past.

Finally a day came when the straw was raked aside, the brick walls were hacked open, and the crate once again exposed. With a squeal of wrenched nails, the lid was pulled off. The bundle was lifted out of the crate and the yards and yards of fabric unwound from her form, and the black goddess was once again visible to the world. A breeze blew across her belly and her eyes opened for the first time in two centuries onto the astonished Brahmins and their wives and children. None of them had ever seen her, and with gasps they fell in worship before her. Again they washed her, fed her, ornamented her.

And then they fell to quarreling. As she stood in the field beside their house, the angry voices of men argued about ancestors and bloodlines and property and household divisions. Her eyes, fixed over their heads, rested on the ancient hills and a stream that endlessly flowed down toward the great river. Where is that sage who first sang of me, she wondered. How I miss him! The quarreling did not stop, and she, the slayer of demons, began to seethe. These who have unearthed me are unworthy heirs of their ancestors.

They grow tiresome. I think I will go elsewhere, she decided impulsively.

It was in the black of night, after the Brahmins and their families were asleep. 'Ping,' went the black marble of her raised left heel, and a piece fell to the ground.

Both feet still played on the prone form of her consort, and the foot was still connected to her leg by a thin stretch of stone, but a chunk the length of a child's forearm containing the heel was broken off.

In the morning, when the Brahmin wife came with a hibiscus blossom to worship her, she gasped to see the damage to the black goddess's leg. She called her husband and they searched everywhere, and confronted the servants and villagers, but no trace of the missing heel was ever found.

CHAPTER 1

MYSTFIRE

B ored, Annie clicked the Facebook icon to see what her so-called friends were up to. She had to admit most of these weren't exactly friends so much as acquaintances she had picked up over the course of a (fairly long) lifetime. They kept turning up and hooking into this brand-new network of daily likes and comments. Now that they were once again a part of daily life, she hardly knew what to do with them. If she had really wanted to keep those long-lost high school friendships she could have kept current with them during all those decades they were marrying, babying, working, divorcing, and starting over again. She didn't then, and didn't really now, either.

She wrote: "Saw my doctor today. Started me on statins! Whoa! Am I ready for this?"

A long-ago friend who must have been online at that very moment appeared almost instantly: "I know what you mean! I've been on them for a year already!"

Half an hour later there were three "likes."

It wasn't enough to fill the quiet days now that she had retired, early, to make space for a new phase of life to begin. Finding old friends was turning back, not moving forward, but it was a lot easier. She stared at her computer screen, as if the answer were just there someplace, a URL away.

The screen on her MacBook Pro faded; she tapped it awake again.

In the next room, her husband was turning off the television. She could hear him lift himself out of his chair and wander into the kitchen, yawning loudly. The refrigerator door opened. After a few minutes it closed. The faucet ran, a glass filled with water.

"You coming?" he said from the kitchen.

Just before bed, after brushing her teeth but not flossing, she took the first statin. This was the time each day when she examined herself in the mirror. She felt she had a still servicible face. The bathroom lights were kind, the very best available view of her these days. She had good bones, people said, and nice blue eyes. People used to say she looked like Candice Bergen, who was born the same year she was. She doesn't look much like the young Candice any more, but what does Candice look like now? She kept her still-blonde hair cut boyishly short, with thick bangs falling low along her forehead. She pulled the strands in front of her ears toward her cheeks, then pushed them back behind her ears. Tomorrow she was getting the back of her neck shaved and a trim of the front, which was getting a little long.

She crawled into bed beside Ted, and turned out the lights. Their nightly routine proceeded:

"Night, Ted."

"G'night."

Tomorrow morning she had to take the next statin. Lying in bed, with the lights out, the brief satisfaction of a few moments ago slipped away. She felt whispers of old age with the beginning of pill-taking. Medicare would be paying for the bone density test her doctor recommended, and he was insisting on a colonoscopy. In his office she had promised she would, but I'm never doing that, she vowed to herself in the dark.

The skylight over her bed opened onto a sky shining with a full moon. Each night, if the moon was full and the sky clear, it appeared on the right side of the skylight and drifted gently to the left, then disappeared, leaving a silver wake on the edges of the window and on the armoire on the other side of the room. By then, if all went well, she was asleep.

An hour later, she was still staring out the skylight, listening to Ted's deep breathing and a gentle sighing from the broadleaf maples in the yard. The silver had vanished from the night sky and clouds had moved in. She got up and tiptoed downstairs. In the middle of the night, it wasn't your world any more. It belonged to the raccoons who crept up the bank from the bay to munch oysters on your deck and drop speckled poop on the stairs. It belonged to the owl hooting from the woods and to the ducks stirring in their sleep at the water's edge. Creatures rustled in the shrubbery and pounced on other creatures that cried out in fear. She loved to quietly eavesdrop on this other world from her deck in the middle of the night.

Half an hour later she was at her laptop, still in the dark. On Facebook, there were five more likes and one more comment. "Oh, God! We're getting old!" Diane said. She remembered Diane as a vivacious black-haired flirt in college, but she could tell from her photo that she had lost the black curls and put on a hundred pounds. Diane had grandkids that regularly left encouraging posts: "Get a life, Grandma!" said her granddaughter, Sara. Sara's twin, Josh, wrote: "Grandma, why don't you take up WOW?"

Annie googled WOW. It opened onto a page of startling molten blackness with a fire-breathing dragon warning: "A New Age Has Begun." It promised a ten day free trial. Later, she couldn't say what had overtaken her, actually. Maybe the dragon seemed a part of the mysterious other world that lived off her deck in the shadows. Maybe it was the promise of a New Age. It took a while for the download to finish, which Annie spent thinking things like, "What is this, a video game?" And "Diane should go on a diet." And listening for Ted to wake up and come down the stairs looking for her.

To play this game you had to invent a new self. Annie instantly got the appeal of this. If only! She could be a human – but why so ordinary? – or an orc. Knowing the Lord of the Rings trilogy by heart, she would never be an orc. Or an undead (euwww) or a dwarf. There were two elf options, and since she liked the looks of the Blood Elves better than the Night Elves, she joined the Horde.

Apparently these races of beings specialized in certain skills. There were hunters, warriors, priests, and others. She tried out the warrior option, and there she was, slashing the air with a broadsword. Not really her, even in some ideal alternate universe. Priest, hands uplifted with some kind of shimmering dust falling through? She'd had enough of priests and pastors in her life. What is a mage? The mage formed a ball of fire in her hand and hurled it into the air. Mage meaning magician, apparently, using fire as a weapon against. . . whatever went on in the World of Warcraft. She gave herself a name – Mystfire – and clicked enter.

Instantly she was swooping through a sunny forest, then through a golden arch and along a paved avenue. She flew past the walls of a city to cross a creek and enter another forest, and was finally deposited outside a shiny pavilion in the woods. Here Annie had a good look at her new self, Mystfire the Blood Elf, slim of waist, gold of hair, a wicked staff strapped across her back. Mystfire waited there, sexy and impatient, first on one foot, then the other. Clearly she was bored, wanted to get going. There was a row of buttons along the bottom of the screen that Annie clicked one by one. Another Blood Elf stood in front of her with an exclamation point over her head. Annie clicked on her and received her first quest.

Over the next three hours, she learned how to run and jump and wield her staff. She figured out how to kill mana wyrms with her fireball, collect loot, sell stuff, and turn in a quest. She had gathered lynx collars, explored Sunstrider Isle, and joined a guild. When she finally crept back up to her bed, Mystfire, the Blood Elf mage, had reached level five. Annie hadn't had this much fun in years.

Back in bed, now 4 AM, her head was full of the bright world beyond her laptop screen. She had gone through the looking glass, silly as it seemed to be running in her mage's robes with her fireball and frostbolt, after mana wyrms and wraiths. She who had just started on statins and was grimly looking retirement full in the face. What was wrong with this picture?

CHAPTER 2

__ A GREAT OPPORTUNITY __

Next morning Annie was awakened by Ted in the shower. Usually she was first up and showered, but if you've spent hours bent over your laptop in the middle of the night, your morning routine isn't going to follow its normal course.

"You're still in bed?" Ted asked, emerging with a towel around his waist. "No coffee yet?" He was annoyed.

"Just getting up. Give me five minutes."

Most mornings over coffee, Ted read the local paper while Annie read the New York Times; the Times was her paper, which Ted refused to read. "Look at this circled item," he said. He handed her the local paper with the real estate section folded open.

Fixer-upper foreclosure. Buy for half its recent sale cost. Best buy in town! Call 253-340-8412

A groan from Annie.

"What?!"

"Not another one!"

"Why not? Can't be a better time."

"I can't face another house project."

"Yes you can." With emphatic finality.

She looked at him hard. "No. I can't." He looked hard back at her. A tense silence filled the sightline between them, implying an old, old fight that they wouldn't actually have to have because the silence said all.

Ted returned to his paper. "We'll just go take a look at it." End of conversation.

Annie took her second statin. Dressed in khaki jeans and a black shirt and sandals, she left the house for her hair appointment, but she had time to stop by Costco. It was a rare sunny day in April and she was feeling good now that she was out of the house and on her own, even though she had no place to go, really, and nothing much to do. The hair trim was make-work, something to keep busy at, but it would only take half an hour. After that maybe she'd get a pedicure at Nguyen's where they have chairs that massage your back while your feet soak in blue water. That's a whole hour of pampering, although you have to watch stupid shows on their wall-mounted television unless you take a book with you. She stopped at Costco to pick up a book because she didn't think to bring one from home. Since Borders closed, Costco was the only bookstore left in town.

The books that hadn't appealed to her yesterday also didn't appeal to her today. She circumambulated the table twice, slowly reading every title. Twice she stopped at "Beginning Programming for Dummies." There was something about beginning something. . . .

How many years of life did she have left? Her grandmother had lived to 101. If Annie lived that long, she had thirty-six more years! It was a shocking number, shocking to think of all the empty days of hair cuts and pedicures, the thousands of statins, to be joined no doubt by other prescriptions, and Medicare procedures her doctor would dream up, and surgeries to fix things that would go wrong, getting weaker because she never did anything, finally pushing a walker around because she was too unsteady on legs unused to having any demands placed on them, until eventually it was easier to stay seated in front of the television, and easier to watch television than to actually think, with nothing really worth thinking about anyway, because who cares what an old lady thinks?

She had to begin something, something big and hard. She picked up "Beginning Programming for Dummies" and headed for the checkout counter.

☆ ☆ ☆

At ten minutes to ten, as she was driving to her hair appointment, the marimba sounded from her bag and she fumbled for her iPhone. It was Ted.

"Annie! We've got an appointment in ten minutes at the house!"

"Unnnn. . . . " She checked her watch. "Sorry, can't make it. I've got a hair appointment."

"Yes you can. Your hair is fine. Meet me at 1527 Junot Street. It's just off Hunthausen before you get to Market. Easy to find. Great location, in fact."

Damn, she thought. Here we go again. It felt like a slide down a chute into a maelstrom that would consist of leaking plumbing, damaged sheetrock, broken steps, smoky windows, and mildew. How many crappy little houses had they bought, fixed up, and flipped? Did they ever actually make any money? Ted wasn't into spreadsheets; he just put charges onto credit cards, then worried about selling the house, and then when he finally did, he used the profit to pay off the maxed out credit cards. Annie had no idea whether they were ahead or behind, and she didn't think Ted knew, either. Now here they went again.

"Ted. . . ," she began, then spluttered.

"Annie, you've got to support me in this."

Supporting her husband was the great moral theme in their life together. Not in the old "help-meet" sense where wives' life purpose is the support their husbands, like the woman from Proverbs whose children rise up to call her blessed. No, Annie supported Ted in the new, psychological sense where claims could be laid on partners who had separate agendas and longed for separate lives, claims authorized by accusations of blame and guilt that would come if you failed to support him. Ted was a master of guilt-giving, while Annie never mastered what might have been an art of turning the tables, using the same language against him. Partly that was because she didn't ask for support, what she wanted was more freedom, more independence, and that was exactly the kind of language that got nowhere, just more blame and guilt for trying to evade the support a loving wife owed her husband.

"Ted, I told you I'm busy. I've got an appointment."

"It's just a hair thing. Do it tomorrow. Do it this afternoon. This is a big deal, Annie. . . the realtor is meeting me here, she's driving up right now, actually, do you want me to make this decision without you?"

Annie certainly did not want that, given how fully it implicated her. Supporting Ted meant throwing herself fully into his projects. She would spend the next six months on this house. She at least wanted a voice at the beginning.

"All right. I'm not excited about this, Ted. It'll take me ten minutes to get there."

The house was a little rambler on a cul-de-sac of similar houses in better condition than it was. That was rule number one for Ted: buy houses that are the worst on their block. From the street it looked all garage, with a wide blacktop driveway filled with cracks from which weeds sprouted. Buttercups and dandelions covered the lawn. She could see Ted and the realtor in the living room through the open front door.

"Hi!" Annie greeted the realtor. She was a young slim woman in a pink suit with a very short skirt and very high heels.

"Hi, Annie is it? Come on in, we're just getting started. This is probably the best deal in town and you are the first party I've shown it to!" She handed Annie a copy of the MLS sheet on the house.

The blue carpet had dark stains by the front door and other unpleasant smudges and creases where heavy furniture had recently sat.

"Obviously this place needs a lot of work. The owners disappeared in the middle of the night, without any clean-up. A crew has been in to cart off trash, but they didn't do any real cleaning. As you can see." They were all looking at the carpet. "A shampoo will do a lot for this."

"Maybe. Or maybe a tear-out," Annie said.

"We want to do minimum fix-up for a quick re-sale," Ted said.

"Absolutely!" At least the realtor was supporting him.

They moved from room to room, through the kitchen nook, into the kitchen itself, where a dirty patch of linoleum was all that remained of the refrigerator. The oven would have to be replaced. The porcelain sink was chipped, and the faucet was cockeyed with gray mineral deposits around the base. In the bedrooms, broken venetian blinds sagged to the floor, and mysterious scuffings covered the walls.

Ted was keeping his opinions to himself, which Annie recognized as the strategy he used to keep realtors from guessing that he was really interested in the property. "Um-huh," was all he'd say. Annie limited her comments to pointing out high-cost and high-labor issues:

"This wallpaper will have to be steamed off before being replaced."

"Not going to be easy to repair this window sill."

"Carpets throughout have to go."

"I'm a little worried about the wiring."

"I don't know if anything can be done about the smell."

☆   ☆   ☆

Back home over lunch, Ted's enthusiasm was on show. Annie was feeling something fluttery in her chest, which might be about the fight she felt coming, or maybe the statins.

"This is a great deal! That house sold for $155,000 just five years ago. Now they are only asking $75,000. Poor suckers bought at the top of the market."

"Right. And who's going to buy it now? Us?"

"I'm going to get it for less. We won't need to put in more than, maybe, ten K, turn around and sell it for, umm, 85-90."

"Who wants that kind of house, even if it's fixed up? People at that end of the market can't get loans any more."

"Well, there are plenty of investors around. . . ."

"Yeah, like us, who want to buy low, fix up, and sell high."

". . . AND renters. If we can't sell it we can rent for a while. THEN sell, when the market comes back."

Annie slowly shook her head.

"You're always so negative!"

"I don't want to do this!"

"You never support me. I have to fight you on everything."

"Here we go again! I ALWAYS support you. We've done six of these. Do we actually make any money?"

"Are you questioning my financial decisions?"

"Well, I might be. Actually, yes I might be."

"Damn!" He pushed back from the table and stood up. It was the worst word he ever used; Annie had much stronger language in her lexicon. "Damn you! I'm sick of this!"

"Ted. . . ."

"Don't Ted me! Everything is a fight with you! What is it with you?" He stomped a circle on the kitchen floor. "For years I've put up with this! You never change! Never, never, never."

Annie was getting worried. "I think you should calm down. Let's leave it for a while. We can talk about it later." It was dangerous to make him mad.

"Fine!" He stormed out the back door and slammed it shut.

Annie went out to the deck where a gentle mist was turning into drizzle. She flung herself into a deck chair under a canopy. She could see where this was headed; it would be a long afternoon. The argument would continue until she caved in and agreed to what he wanted, but until that moment she would hear for the thousandth time the litany of her many failings over all the years since they had married in their early twenties. That was a long, long time for character flaws to pile up. Motherhood and her career had been a sequence of satisfying accomplishments for her, but they had spun off additional items of dissatisfaction for Ted. She had ALMOST let her career trump her own children, as Ted put it. She had been in a graduate program in anthropology after being encouraged to go for her PhD by her professors. But during the spring semester, she got pregnant with her first child, Jennie. Everyone – Ted, his parents, her parents – urged her to think of her family, not just of herself; she should put aside these ambitions for the time being while she had the baby and saw it through its first few years. Later she could go back.

So she did exactly that. She reapplied when Jennie was three, got accepted again, and was just finishing her second year when she got pregnant again. This was Sam. It was now the 1970s, and women had more support from the women's movement to follow their hearts and ambitions. Even Ted could see that maybe a two-income family was not a bad idea, although Annie's chosen career was a bit exotic for a woman with two children. There was talk of fieldwork, a year abroad, and what would happen to the children and Ted then?

But it never got that far. It was interrupted by an indiscretion that stopped her career trajectory and almost destroyed her family. Though it wasn't an actual affair – no sex, no touch – it came close enough that she spent the rest of her life living it down and making amends. After several weeks of violent reactions from Ted – a bloodied lip, several incidents of Annie crouched in a corner with Ted shouting and battering her with the back of his hand – life settled down again. Ted's violence was understood as a fair enough reaction to the emotional suffering she had inflicted, and the actual incident, the almost-affair, became the factual datum of all Ted's blistering condemnations at moments of slack support from his wife. It was the evidence of her weakness of moral fiber, of her psychological instability. It had lighted a terminal fire in Ted's own character, laying a bed of embers that occasionally settled under white ash but never could be extinguished.

The fight was resumed an hour later, it simmered through an angry dinner, and finally, in the early evening, Annie said the words that Ted was waiting for:

"Okay, Ted, maybe we should just get the house."

"No, not if you are really opposed to it."

"Really, if you think it's a good idea, I want to support it."

He didn't say anything more. He watched television for a couple of hours, and then went to bed.

Annie sat on her deck until darkness was fully descended. She drank a glass of red wine, then poured a second one. Aside from noting the restless sounds of the creatures that lived nearby, she did not seem to be thinking about anything. Her mind was empty. This was the form of Zen that got her through life.

Her deck faced the eastern sky, from which, now that the drizzle had stopped and the sky had partially cleared, the cold moon could be seen rising. The waters were ruffled slightly by a night breeze, breaking apart the image of itself the moon cast into the bay. How brightly shine the unreal things that cannot be touched, she thought. Nothing is there in that water but reflected light, as unreal as digital images on a computer screen. Like Mystfire, my fire-hurling alter ego in her purple robe.

That night Mystfire grew in power as she slew wretched urchins and ether fiends. To the sound of cellos in the tranquilizing soundtrack, Annie experienced the power of transformation. Mystfire, her avatar, was rewarded with ever more powerful weapons and spells, frost nova and arcane torrent and fire blast. She rose in distinction with each completed quest. She ventured into new, stranger lands. Annie recognized the absurdity of it all, but couldn't shake the spell.

☆ ☆ ☆

CHAPTER 3

BEGINNING PROGRAMMING
FOR DUMMIES

It was six weeks until the little house on Junot Street closed. Ted and Annie drove by it frequently in anticipation of getting their hands on its unpleasant features, and now and then Annie was even able to apply some creative imagination to the front yard landscaping. But the thought of actually getting back inside that front room filled her with dread.

In the meantime, she worked her way through Beginning Programming for Dummies. Her head was filled with the relative merits of C++, REALbasic, and SQL. She understood sequential, branching, and looping instructions. She downloaded Xcode from Apple's web site for developers. What she couldn't exactly explain to herself was what the point of it all was. Whatever it was, it must be subliminal. She had always had a techie side to her, beginning in the mid-1990s when the high school where she taught had gotten Apple computers with HyperCard for the library and she had led the way with her English class in making programs and getting the students to launch their essays and photos onto the

Internet. Those had been exciting times, but in the meantime the design geniuses had taken over the Internet and she had fallen behind. She hankered to catch up.

When the house at long last closed, Ted's excitement filled the air with his unusual sort of testosterone. It seemed to Annie that run-down empty houses that could be salvaged and brought up to standards were exactly his model of family life. Wives and children were by nature defective human beings that could, with enormous effort, be made acceptable to the world if an alpha male like himself were willing to expend the enormous effort it required. They had to be propped up and repaired; bad parts had to be identified and replaced; they had to submit to his ministrations with gratitude. In the end, perhaps – he didn't ever exactly say this – they could be put on the market and sold.

The day they drove over to pick up the key, Annie wrote on her Facebook page: "Starting new project today. A whole house! Yikes!" She exited before any likes or comments could arrive.

She had a clipboard with the notes they had made from memory of all the tasks they had to face, which went all the way down one and a half sheets of yellow pad and would be updated as they walked through the house for the first time without a realtor in tow.

Annie had taken her statin religiously for all six weeks, morning and night, and she was now certain that the delicate flutters she felt in her chest on a regular basis were due to it. There was an alternate theory, however, that it was dread of the house. She had been having "bad house" dreams, in which she and Ted lived in a series of terrible, terrible houses with uneven dirt floors and dirty plank walls, furnished with old iron stoves and broken down sofas. She woke from these dreams grateful for her lovely home on the bay with its inviting deck. For once, life was better than dreams.

Ted turned the key in the lock, tugged and shoved, and pushed the door in over the blue carpet. A shock of mildew or cat shit puffed out. Annie gasped and halted. Ted stepped forward, she stepped back.

She felt her heart stop, her lungs empty. If she entered this house with Ted, she wouldn't be able to breathe. She would pass out, there on the filthy blue carpet, and never come round again. Dizzy and nauseated, she backed away from the house and from Ted. He hadn't noticed she wasn't behind him as he stepped forward, taking possession of the house. Not until he heard the ignition turn and the engine roar did he look out the window in time to see Annie drive away.

"What the f. . . ?!" he said.

At home, Annie grabbed a suitcase and began tossing underwear and clothes into it. Some kind of panic had overtaken her. She scooped makeup and jewelry into a smaller bag. She yanked open the bottle of statin and dumped it into the toilet. If she didn't do this now, she never would. But what was it she was doing? She grabbed Beginning Programming for Dummies and her laptop and dashed for the car; at the door, she stopped and ran back for her passport in the top drawer of her desk. Fifteen minutes later, as her cellphone hysterically registered call after call and text after text, Annie was on her way out of town.

She was in the car on the freeway in the middle of a cloudy day, it was getting ready to rain, and she didn't know where she was going. Her heart was racing. She had to stop someplace where she could calm down and think things through, and she had to make the phone stop ringing.

She saw the exit to Dash Point, and soon found herself at the state park where they occasionally had brought the kids when they were little. Jen and Sam had loved to stomp in the sandy muck at low tide and run along the driftwood without falling off. There was a covered area with barbecue stands and picnic tables chained in place. She sat on one of the tables, damp even under the sheltering roof.

She pulled her iPhone out of her bag and set it on vibrate. She didn't want to be reached by Ted. His demands on her, even at a distance through her cell phone, made her shudder. She knew exactly what his voice was going to sound like when he finally reached her. What do you think you're doing? he'd demand. Explain yourself. At that, all her speech centers would shut down. She wouldn't be able to explain, or to say anything lucid at all, and this would infuriate him. She knew exactly how the house conversation would go: You're walking away JUST when we've committed ourselves to this house?! If you didn't want to do it, why didn't you say something before now? Are you crazy?! He seemed to grow two sizes when he was mad.

The rain started, making soft taps as it splattered on the mossy shingles of the roof. The tide was half-way in, and the far shore was a line of black-green forest. Annie felt oddly self-contained in this solitary space, a single deer in the forest.

What do I do now? She had her car, she had two checks that came automatically every month, and she had the future. There was not even a tiny sensible part of her that looked back at the comfortable house where her life with Ted went on. A growing excitement seized her: I can leave that. I don't need it. I can do something else with the rest of my life. She was going forward, not back.

✵ ✵ ✵

It took an hour to reach the university district, which she spent mentally writing rules for her new life.

First: Don't go back. You'll never get another chance.

Second: Ted's anger is going to turn to grief. This is a cruel thing to do to him.

Third: He needs to start over, too.

Fourth: "Get a life." Yes!

Fifth: How do you do that, exactly?

These were sequence instructions and loop instructions. She went over them and over them, but it took a while to find the next line:

Sixth: Get in touch with Karen.

Before long she was looking for a parking spot in front of Taverna on the Ave. Taverna was a Greek restaurant where she and several friends used to have lunch during her second year in graduate school, before she got pregnant with Sam. Getting lucky, she found a spot right in front and went in. Nothing had changed; the same dusty plastic grape vines winding round the wine cellar; the same bright lights and small tables. She took her old one in the window and ordered a plate of feta and olives, plus a glass of red wine. She placed her iPhone face down on the table, where it periodically shivered with desperate calls from Ted. Each time, she picked it up, saw who was calling, and put it back down.

Karen Andersen was her best friend from university days, but their lives had moved apart after Annie dropped out to have Sam. Unlike Annie, Karen kept on, went on to do fieldwork in India, earn her PhD, and get a job as a professor at the same university. Annie followed Karen's career with interest – no, with frank jealousy – as she herself got a teaching certificate and prepared to spend her life with high school students. Karen wrote a book about her fieldwork that Annie read with a constant pain in her stomach, while she wrote lesson plans on imagery and symbolism in literature and graded first and second drafts of teen-age essays.

Karen married Bob Hansen, a political scientist, and for a few years the two of them would invite Annie and Ted to their Christmas parties and summer barbecues, but Ted didn't like these affairs or the air of superiority he thought he experienced from Karen and Bob, and finally it just became easier to send regrets when invitations came. She hadn't seen Karen for ten years.

The iPhone shivered again, and this time it was Jennie. Annie stared at the name while debating whether to answer. She didn't want to make an accounting of herself yet. But she didn't want the whole family to imagine her lying in a ditch or tied up in a barn and then calling the police.

"Hi, Jennie."

"Mom! What's up? Where ARE you? Dad's frantic!"

"Jennie. . . "

"Are you okay, Mom?"

Annie could hear the alarm in Jennie's voice that would be the result of Ted's wild guesses about her sanity. "Jennie, listen. I am fine. You have to believe me. I am going to be out of touch for a little while, but believe me, I'm a big girl and I can take care of myself. It might be better if you don't talk to Dad about me. You should certainly be supportive of him. . ." she was shifting this responsibility to Jennie, ". . .but don't accept any of his ideas about me because he DOESN'T KNOW WHAT'S GOING ON. Do you hear that?"

Long pause.

"Yeah, Mom. I think I get it."

"Okay. Good. I'll be in touch before long. REALLY, don't worry about me."

"Okay Mom. I love you."

"I love you too, Sweetheart. Bye."

Seventh: Brief, firm message of reassurance to family.

Eighth: Followed by radio silence.

Next, she thumbed around on her iPhone until she produced a phone number for Karen. She touched dial. Soon, "Hello?"

"Hi, Karen. It's Annie." All casual and warm old friendship.

"Annie! Hey! Great to hear from you. Just out of the blue like this!"

"Well, I'm in the city, eating at Taverna, actually, and I thought I'd give you a call. Must be the feta and olives that did it."

"Haha. I'm so sure. How long are you here?"

"Oh, a few days, maybe. I'm staying at the Holiday Inn, but I hope we can get together before I leave."

"Are you alone? Why don't you stay with me? I've got a spare bedroom. Then we can get all caught up."

And that was how Annie came to be ringing a doorbell at a fine old arts and crafts bungalow on Capitol Hill.

☆ ☆ ☆

Karen still wore her hair in the same smooth Scandinavian page tucked behind her ears and the same turtleneck sweater, sleeves pulled up, that Annie always remembered. Because it was evening, she wore it over jeans. She exclaimed with pleasure to see Annie at the door, pulled her in, gave her a warm hug, and sat her down on the sofa with a glass of white wine. "I'm SO glad to see you!"

Karen's living room, with bleached wooden floors and mullioned windows, had the same spare lines that Karen herself had. Framed photographs on the walls depicted scenes from the places in India where Karen had worked, and there was a Shiva Nataraja on the mantle, but aside from those mementoes, it was a room where a woman lived with books and friends and simple comforts. Annie felt the contrast to her beloved house on the bay, its interior decor expressing only the confused and predictable character of people who did most of their shopping at Costco.

"You look terrific! You still look like Candice Bergen!"

"Oh sure! If only! I haven't had my hair trimmed in six weeks."

"Keep this length. I remember the long golden hair from years ago. Remember? Big earrings, long braid. Very cool."

"Yeah. . . ."

"Now, catch me up. What's going on with you? What's brought you here?"

"Karen, I think I've run away from home." Annie immediately wanted the words back, but there they were, pathetically loose in the air of Karen's orderly living room. She quickly corrected: "That is, I've decided to change course. I've left Ted and I'm not going back."

"Wow. This is a big deal." Karen looked at Annie admiringly. "Well, finally. I never could understand that relationship. You gave up so much and he treated you so . . . disrespectfully. I always thought so. Annie, you'll find that when you finally take such a step, your friends don't disapprove like you fear. They don't think you are crazy. More likely they wonder why it took you such a very long time. What finally brought you to this?"

"I guess it was the flip-house."

"Flip house?"

"The fixer-upper he wanted to buy and flip. You wouldn't believe this house!" Annie began describing the house that she and Ted has just bought as their latest joint project, and before long they were both laughing so wickedly that they had to set their glasses down. "Sky blue sculpted carpets with cat shit! Orange stains in the toilet bowl! Fist punches in the sheet rock!"

"Such a deal! How can you walk away from this opportunity! All the money."

Yes, there was that, Annie thought. "Well, there will be some financial consequences I'll have to face."

"Yes! It's the financial consequences that hold people in place. If you are really determined, you have to keep your priorities straight."

"Well I do have my own income, now that I've retired. And some things I'd like to do."

"Yeessss? Such as?"

"Don't think I'm crazy. I know I don't fit the profile. But I want to learn computer programming."

Karen's jaw opened and stuck there.

"This probably sounds crazy. I know this is for twenty year old dudes, but I refuse to accept that gender stereotype."

"You want to get a job at Microsoft?" They both laughed.

"Well not at first." They laughed again. "I want to do something HARD. Something that really takes some energy and brain power. I've wasted so much of my life on easy work and making people happy. Or, trying to make them happy."

"Teaching high school was not meaningless work, Annie. Don't disparage yourself."

"I don't mean that. I just mean, that part of my life is over and now I'm on to the next part. I can't look back. And the one thing I can think of that I'd like to do is get into the computer science program at the university."

"Ooooh." Karen tried not to turn her face into a downer for Annie, but she knew the university well. "That's tough, you know. That's really tough. Have you checked out their website? All those math and science courses along with the programming ones. And it takes four years."

Annie nodded soberly. "Well, I've made a start. I've completed Beginning Programming for Dummies!" This provoked more uncontrolled girly laughter. "And I'm going to start realistically. Anyone can learn how to make a website." She went on to describe a project she had in mind, a site where women could go to tell their personal stories and meet other women with shared interests. It would be like Facebook, but with depth. Twitter with no word limit. Karen thought this was a very cool idea.

"There are software programs that you can easily learn to help you with that." After a pause, Karen leaned toward Annie. "Bob and I have split up, you know."

"No. I haven't heard."

"Yes. In our case, it was because of a sexy graduate student of his. I was angry at first, but to tell you the truth, I have a better life now and we are still friends. Men need women more than women need men. Of course, I still have my salary and position, which makes a big difference. But I like being single. I love my freedom!"

"It won't be like that with Ted and me. I won't escape easily."

"No. He has a different personality type. He's controlling and needy. And mean."

"I should have done this long ago. Then he'd have remarried and I'd have had a different life."

"Not too late for either of those things."

"Hard to imagine him remarrying, but it would be the best thing for him."

"I think there should be time limits on marriage. Five year contracts, then they run out. Make it a lot of work to renew them."

"Yeah. You'd have to petition a judge, who would listen to your arguments and have to decide whether you should be allowed to go on."

"And your kids would understand that there's a big exciting change coming in a certain year. They'd be taught to look forward to it."

"Uh-huh. Kids like change so much!" She thought about Jennie's call. Now in her twenties, Jennie just might understand. But ten-fifteen years ago, it would have been a different story. Although if she had left with Jennie back when she was two or three at the time everything had exploded, she could have carried on with her original career and have lived a completely different life.

"By the way," said Karen, "guess what David is doing now?"

"David?" Just out of the blue, that name. "What?"

At that moment her iPhone vibrated. Annie glanced at it and saw it was Jennie. She decided not to answer it.

"David is now working for the World Bank."

Ping-ping. A text message arrived: "Mom, please pick up! I have to talk to you!" Annie sighed. It was not going to be easy to drop out of sight. She called Jennie back and heard her daughter's voice, in tears.

"Mom, Dad's going crazy! I don't know what to do. He's saying terrible things about you. He's going to get you committed because you are mentally unstable. He's going to get even. He called you a whore and a bitch! He said you never loved us. I've never seen him like this! I don't know what to do." She burst into sobs.

"Oh, Jennie. . . ."

Karen's phone rang, and Karen went to the side table to answer it.

"Jennie, he'll get over this. This is just the first day. What have you said to him? Did you tell him you talked to me?"

On Karen's phone, it was Ted. "Karen. Ted Gilbert. Have you heard from Annie today?"

"Ted!" she exclaimed, truly surprised, and wanting to send a warning to Annie. "Why, what a surprise to hear from you."

Annie went on talking to Jenny. "Jenny, please try to calm down. You know your father; he's noisy and reactive when he gets upset. Don't listen to the things he's saying right now. He knows they aren't true."

On the other phone, Ted to Karen: "Don't lie to me, Karen. I know she's there. I hear her talking."

"Ted, I don't know what you're talking about. I haven't heard from Annie for years." She hung up.

"Jenny, where are you? Are you at the house?"

"Yes."

"Go home. Go back to your apartment. Call Kit and Julie to come over and spend the night with you. You don't have to handle this."

"Okay, Mom," said Jennie in her old little girl voice. "Mom, I'm worried about you."

"Sweetheart, right now I'm worried about you. Please, this is something I just have to do. I'm so, so sorry if I am hurting you in the process."

"I want to see you."

"We will definitely see each other soon. I love you. Now please go on home." They hung up.

To Karen: "Did I hear what I thought I heard?"

"Yes, he knows you're here."

"How could he have guessed? It never crossed my mind to come here until I was sitting at the Taverna. Of course he always says he knows me better than I know myself. He knows what I'm thinking before I know it."

They were both wondering the same thing; what would Ted do now? Would he come here? They talked for a while about what to do next, whether Ted was on his way to them, whether he was dangerous, whether he would have a gun, should they call the police? Would it be better if Annie went back to the hotel, or would that leave Karen alone and at greater risk? Maybe Annie was wrong to just walk out without a word, her only message the empty drawers and closet at home. Surely the man she had spent her life with deserved more explanation than this.

She decided to send a single email message. She wouldn't tell him immediately that the marriage was dead. That was too blunt. If she let him know it was on life support and may not survive, he could start getting used to the idea. In Karen's spare bedroom, she turned on her Mac and wrote to him:

Dear Ted,

I'm sorry to do this to you. We've spent thirty years together, I changed my career for you. We've raised two beautiful children. But I now need to re-think the meaning of my life. You should do the same thing. I need some space. I don't want to get together and talk about it. Please don't try to contact me. I'll be in touch when I've decided what to do. Annie

☆ ☆ ☆

Chapter 4

_____ A Strange Stone _____

Annie was waiting at the front door of Bank of America, university branch, at 9AM when it opened for business. At 9:02 she was relieved to find that their entire life savings of $50,350 was still there. She withdrew $25,175 of it and left the bank. (At 9:08 Ted discovered that Annie had beat him to it.) Annie walked a block and a half to Chase, where she opened an account and deposited her share of the Gilberts' life savings. While there, the young clerk was happy to establish a new MasterCard account in her name only. Back at Karen's house, she spent the rest of the morning figuring out how to redirect the direct deposits of her two monthly retirement checks to the new account.

Karen came in at 11AM with two Starbucks lattes and two blueberry scones. "We have to talk," she said, as they cosied up around her small patio table in a nest of potted plants. "I think you've got to get away."

"I just did!" Annie laughed, in a really terrific mood, given the morning's financial triumphs.

"Yes, but you are still within reach, and I think you're going to be having a really angry visitor today. You are in no position to face up to that right now. Are you?"

Although feeling strong and free for the moment, Annie knew how quickly it would dissolve into guilt and humiliation if Ted showed up at the door. "Have you got a suggestion?"

"Yes, as a matter of fact. I have friends in India. You were going to go there once, as I recall." Indeed! They had taken Hindi together for two years, until Annie dropped out to have Sam. Karen took a third year, then went to India where she became fluent over the course of the following year of fieldwork. Annie tried to hold on to her rudimentary knowledge, but it had never been good enough for anything beyond structured classroom conversations, and so it quickly passed into oblivion.

"India!"

"Are you interested?"

"Yes!"

"Do you have a passport?"

"Sure."

"Do you want to go? It's not an easy place. You might hate it."

But Annie was back on the unfinished project of twenty-five years ago. How right it seemed, to pick up the thread of her life twenty-five years later. She started to choke up; her eyes watered. "Sorry, I guess I'm a little emotional. India's a big place; I've tried to get there my whole life, it seems. Have you got any recommendations?"

"I was thinking you could go to an ashram, where you could stay very inexpensively. . . if you were willing to take Hinduism seriously. A really wonderful place, from my point of view, is Rishikesh. I have a lot of contacts there."

They talked the next few hours away, working out details, making notes of names, phone numbers, email addresses, routes, and airplane flights. There was no reason not to go as soon as possible. Annie saw that she was still on the run, that only time and distance would break the bond to Ted. Even more, it would take a radical restructuring inside her head to break the constraints of obligation and honor that had kept her locked in an unhappy marriage for so many years.

That evening they were again sitting at the sheltered patio table under a gentle rain, a bottle of red Demestica from Taverna in front of them.

"Annie, I've got a confession to make. When I suggested you go to India, while it was MOSTLY for your sake, I admit I had an ulterior motive."

Annie took a sip of wine while eyeing her friend.

"I'd go myself, if I didn't have classes going on. Here's the situation. Last year I was working in Rishikesh and the nearby towns of Haridwar and Dehra Dun, visiting ashrams and getting to know women ascetics. There are some great women, all ages, each with her own amazing story. You wouldn't believe it. You'd love to get to know these women, Annie. Most of them are living in collective religious retreats, called ashrams — well, you know that — and most of them have male heads who have all the power. So patriarchy reigns, even there. Now and then you find women in control, but not usually.

"Well, one young woman, Shobha was her name, was particularly intriguing. She was in her early twenties, very beautiful, sombre, lovely sad eyes. There was something about her I couldn't quickly understand. At first, she didn't want to talk to me, although that's not so unusual. They are supposed to be focused on inner spiritual growth and renunciation of the outside world, so when a foreigner comes along wanting to hear their story, that's the opposite of what they are really about. That's ego that pulls them back into the world and away from their spiritual goals. So she was reluctant to talk to me, maybe more reluctant than most." Karen stopped to take several more sips of wine and to remember Shobha.

"But I persisted, and eventually we became good friends. Shobha told me her story. Two years before we met, she was still living at home with her family. They were busy trying to find a husband for her, talking about it with everyone, including the family guru, who came to visit them regularly. This was a wealthy family in Dehra Dun, the kind who would have a guru who took a special interest in them. Shobha had a real spiritual streak. She dreaded the marriage the family was working on, and this made her all the more spiritual. She worshipped the family guru, who has an ashram in Rishikesh. She yearned to devote her life to meditation and a simple discipline of service to the ashram and to the guru."

"She was in love with him?"

"Well we might think of that immediately. If so, it was all sublimated in genuine spiritual yearning that did focus on the person of the guru. She said she'd hear him calling her in the night. She'd leave her bed and long to go to him."

"Wow."

"Yes. And once she did go stumbling out the house on the road to Rishikesh, maybe in some kind of trance. In the morning, they sent servants searching for her, and they found her actually half way there. It was quite dangerous; she could have been raped and murdered. They were quite alarmed.

"Probably they didn't handle it well. Her father is a powerful alpha male type, a bit like Ted, who easily went into rages and terrorized the whole family. You can imagine why she dreaded marriage. He swore she'd never go into an ashram; she'd never live near the guru. He'd be damned if she'd escape from marrying the young guy they'd already found, from another important family in Delhi. She was going to go to Delhi and be a good, rich wife with every possible luxury; how could she not want that? Well, she didn't."

Annie was spellbound, but in the back of her mind floated a further development on her website idea, a place where women from all over the world could tell their stories to other women. She wanted to meet Shobha and get her story launched.

"There was another episode of running away to the guru in the middle of the night. Again they found her, at about the same spot on the road, cut and bruised from a fall. A farmer in a sugar cane cart had come on her at dawn, put her into his cart, and took her to the police station. The police could see she was not a girl to be taken advantage of – which might well have happened to another girl – that she was from an important family. In the scene that ensued back home, her father raging as usual, she described hearing her guru calling to her in the night; that was why she had gone. She described her father's fury. He'd kill her before letting her lead the life she seemed to want.

"But somehow, others in the family slowly calmed him down. Maybe God was calling their daughter, her mother reasoned. Actually, in their case, it was the goddess they suspected might be calling her. This was a *shakt* family, they worshipped Kali. A family doesn't want to cross the desires of the family goddess. Her father began to think through what this might lead to down the road, up against an angry goddess!"

"Go, Kali!" Annie laughed.

"Yeah! Really! So, to finish the story, he finally relented. He allowed her to enter the ashram, where every day she sits at the feet of her guru, who is also a devotee of divine Kali."

"Incredible story."

"Now, here comes the next part. That involves you, maybe. Shobha and I did eventually become good friends, but it took a while. Of course I was very interested in her devotional life, the ascetic discipline that was the center of it. She had her own little shrine in her room for when she wasn't meditating at the main one where everyone worshipped. There was this cheap polychrome picture of Kali thumbtacked to the wall. It looked like calendar art, or goddess pinups. It always surprises me how tacky these pictures can be, but that's what she worshipped. But there were other, smaller deities sitting in front of it on a little tray. These were cheap little pottery things, all covered in red *sindur* that she sprinkled on them, and ash from burned down incense. One of these objects was really just a rock. It was about ten inches high, it came to a peak at the top and had a wide base, probably six inches wide. Vaguely triangular."

"Hmmm."

"Right! You remember some of those readings from our Popular Hinduism seminar. Sure enough, this was the most powerful goddess of all. It belonged to her family, and they had sent it along with her to the ashram, where it seemed she was supposed to be the main family mediator with the goddess. The family reluctantly accepted this alternate role for her, their woman at court, so to speak. The court of the goddess.

"This stone goddess had a story, as well. Back in the ancestral village of Shobha's father, somewhere to the west of Dehra Dun where they now live, they had started out as prosperous landowners, with many acres and fields. They needed a pond to collect water for their cows and water buffalo, so they paid a crew to dig one. You see these man-made ponds everywhere. Well, the workers uncovered this rock. Apparently, as soon as they saw it, work stopped and everyone gathered around to look at it in astonishment and reverence. They sent for the landowner, Shobha's ancestor, and he sent for a Brahmin. The Brahmin announced that the stone was certainly the goddess herself, the most powerful kind, because she shows up on her own, as if on a whim. That night the Brahmin had a dream, in which the goddess Kali appeared to him to say that she had come all the way from Kamakhya Temple looking for her consort. Kamakya Temple is in Assam, all the way across North India, a famous goddess temple. They couldn't believe their good fortune. They took this stone who was really Kali and installed it in their house. And then when Shobha went to the ashram, they sent it with her to protect her. And for her to be responsible for."

"This involves me somehow?"

"Yes. Because I have it here in the house and I need you to take it back."

"What?!?"

Karen went back into the house, letting the screen door slam behind her. A noisy drawer could be heard being pulled open in the bedroom, then Karen reappeared with a package wrapped in red cloth and tied with jute string. The stone was exactly as she had described it. It appeared to be black marble, very irregular in shape but vaguely triangular, with thick coatings of red and gray substances from years of veneration. Its edges seemed smooth and almost curved along one side, with a more jagged edge along another.

"Could it have once been part of a carved image?" Annie wondered.

"It looks like it might have been, doesn't it?" Karen nodded, and pointed to one particularly smooth section of the base. "I've sometimes imagined it might be a bit of arm or leg from a stone image. You know how the Muslim conquerors destroyed 'idols' in the thirteenth century. You see Buddhist and Hindu images with their noses and heads knocked off all the time. Well, we'll never know, but it's interesting to think it was maybe a goddess then, and still is."

They sat there for a while contemplating this ancient deity. It exuded evocative smells, of sandalwood and ferrous soil and something acrid, like kerosene.

"Why is it here?"

"Well, now we're at the end of the story. At least, the end so far. This goddess no doubt has a long way to go beyond her present unusual location. Toward the end of my fieldwork last year – it was August already, and I had classes beginning at the university in September – as I was beginning to make my goodbyes and pack my suitcases, Shobha came to my room very late at night."

"As is her wont."

"Ha! Yes. She was dressed in her usual white sari, given her novice status, but had a backpack on. That looked a little weird. 'Sister,' she said, as she always called me. 'You must do something for me.' She took off the backpack and pulled out this bundle, exactly as you've seen it. 'Please take this with you. But you must promise to bring it back next time you come.' I was shocked, really! This was more than a gift of a bangle to bring a friend back again, a nice little symbol of friendship. 'Shobha, I can't! It's too precious.' She said, 'That's exactly why you must do it. I am worried about it. I am responsible for keeping it safe. It would be safer in America than in Rishikesh right now.' 'Why?' I asked. 'Sister, don't ask me now. When you bring it back, I will be able to clear it up. I'll tell you the whole story. But it must go to safekeeping now.' She gave me a rare beautiful smile. She really looked like a goddess herself. To tell you the truth, it was exciting to think of having it with me for a while, to take it back to my house. I'm not much of a buyer of treasures when I travel. Too much junk that accumulates and your house starts to look like Pier One. But this was special. A real, living goddess."

Annie tilted her head. "You believe that?"

"Well, I don't know what I believe. But the weight of opinion is certainly on their side."

They both turned to look at the triangular rock again. It wasn't sending out any rays, it wasn't emitting any signals. It was silent, in character with itself.

"End of story: a few weeks ago I had an email from a Western friend who lives in Rishikesh. She's Danish like myself, actually. She said she had received a message from Shobha urging her to contact me about something in my possession which she needed back again as soon as possible. Shobha seemed to think I was coming back this summer. I might have left her with the impression that I might do that, but it hasn't worked out. So. . . I'm hoping you will do this thing for me."

CHAPTER 5

_____ MIDDLE SEAT _____

It wasn't going to be a nice flight. Since Annie was determined to leave *tomorrow* – in keeping with her new spirit of impulsiveness -, she was looking at two stops, her choice of San Francisco and Frankfurt, or Toronto and Zurich. She picked the cheapest and printed out her boarding pass for morning. She had a middle seat for all twenty-four hours, plus or minus the time zone difference.

She re-packed the suitcases with all the same clothes from two days ago, except for a ten-inch red object tucked neatly between her underwear and her makeup case. She parked her car on a leafy street two blocks away, and brought the keys back to Karen.

"If there's any hassle about the car, call Jen to come and get it. But I'd rather leave it there for when I get back. Whenever that will be."

She called a taxi, gave Karen a hug and a quick "Thanks a million!" and headed for the airport.

Impatiently enduring the crush in the security line, she saw Ted everywhere, pulling suitcases to every gate, eyeing her over newspapers, furtively drinking beer at AirPub, waiting at Gate 17 for his section of the passenger compartment to be called. In the end, she got herself settled into her narrow middle seat without a confrontation of any kind.

Beside her on the aisle, a large young man in sweatpants read a Hindi phrasebook alternately with drowsing off and ordering club sodas from the drinks cart. On the other side, a young Indian woman slept with her head wedged between the seat back and the window. Presumably she didn't need to work on her Hindi. Annie, who emphatically did, instead had her laptop out working on a different language. She had saved her own Facebook page to her desktop so she could access it in flight. She opened to it as soon as permission came from the flight staff, and then went to View Source. She read:

<!DOCTYPE html PUBLIC "-//W3C//DTD XHTML 1.0 Strict//EN"
"http://www.w3.org/TR/xhtml1/DTD/xhtml1-strict.dtd"><html xmlns="http://www.w3.org/1999/xhtml" xml:lang="en" lang="en" id="facebook" class="no_js">

She was determined to master this language. Was this what Mark Zuckerberg was typing away at as he sat at his desk in his Harvard dorm room? She had seen Social Network twice. It was so inspirational! She had also downloaded a tutorial for learning html, so she opened that in a second screen. The first line of her Facebook code started to make a little sense, at least until she came to "DTD XHTML 1.0 Strict//EN." Did that mean FB used another kind of html, the 1.0 version (strictly!) and in English? There was so much to learn! It was infuriating that it was so impossible to get a decent education after a certain age.

This unexpected turn her life had taken required a kind of planning she had never had to do. She was going to a foreign country for an open-ended stay. All by herself she had to get to Rishikesh, which was somewhere north of New Delhi, and find a place to live, someplace cheap and bearable. Her middle class comforts were a casualty of her impulsive decision to get out of her life. She was willing to trade those comforts for almost anything that wasn't her life with Ted. She was surprised at herself, really, that such a radical leap had been coiling in her subconscious all those years, waiting to spring.

She did have something of a plan. The main goal for the long term was to settle into a place where, for maybe a year, she could study computer programming and learn the software programs that would enable her to launch her website. She thought she could do this with access to the internet and perhaps some books she assumed could be purchased in a major world capital, since there had not been time to do it in Seattle. Beyond this, it would be a year of re-making herself, clearing her mind of years of belittling and guilt. She had no interest in finding a therapist to listen to her stories, exonerate her, and help her find new patterns of response. She had had enough of psychology, after thirty years with Ted. This was something she was determined to do on her own.

For the short term, she had to find Shobha and give her back the stone. Karen had written down the name of the ashram where she lived, Bhav Dham, and the guru who was its head and chief charismatic leader, Swami Shaktinandan Acharya. Karen suggested it might be possible to get a room at this place, if Annie were willing to participate in the worship life of the ashram for a while. The swami made himself available every morning to followers who lived elsewhere, and that was the only way for Annie to get permission to stay there. She would have to go to his audiences – they were called *darshan* – , sit there reverently, and copy what others were doing. Under no circumstance was she to give the package to the swami to pass on to Shobha; it had to go into Shobha's hands personally. And access to Shobha could only be through her guru, this same swami.

But why had Shobha given the stone to Karen in the first place? Why had she wanted it to "go to America"? To be safe, that's what she said. It was a way of hiding it, Annie supposed. A young woman living in an ashram with other devotees under the authority of a controlling master would not have much privacy or personal space to keep her belongings safe, especially since the point of it all was to renounce the material world. But a stone which was really a goddess hardly fit that category; couldn't it be right out in the open, an object of veneration? Maybe it was SO venerated that someone else wanted it. Maybe she was afraid it was going to be stolen. Now, whatever the risk had been, it was over, and she wanted it back. Maybe some rival had left the ashram. Whatever the story was, Annie wanted to meet Shobha and hear it.

✳ ✳ ✳

Flights from the West Coast of the United States always arrive in New Delhi in the middle of the night. Annie was not prepared for the shock of a May night in North India. Exiting from the icy arrival hall, she gasped for air as her lungs filled with steam. She could practically see the heat and feel the sticky aroma of earth and diesel fumes on her skin.

There was a crowd on hand already vying for the dollars and euros of arriving passengers. A man with an enormous belly accosted her. "Madam, where you go? I take you, chip." She shook her head, he shrugged and disappeared.

"You got hotel, Madam? I have good one for you. Very clean, low price." This sweaty-faced man grabbed her two suitcases and headed into the street where every kind of unsavory vehicle jostled for space.

"No! Put those down!"

"Madam, I give you good price on taxi. What you pay?"

"Put them down!"

No one seemed to be in charge. If there was some system in place, it was imperceptible to her.

"Where you from, Madam? Lawn-dawn? Um-reeka? I have family both places. You know Chick-kago?"

"Put. Them. Down."

He finally relinquished her luggage and turned toward another bewildered passenger from Annie's flight. Annie spotted a shiny clean BMW pulled up at the curb. Was it available? The uniformed driver was holding a placard with a name scribbled on it. He was no doubt despatched by one of New Delhi's luxury hotels for someone important traveling on an expense account. Annie had made a reservation at the Green Hotel which was definitely "chip" but came highly recommended on Travelocity. The BMW was not for her.

A polite man in a turban, a Sikh, approached her next, and because he seemed courteous and honest she took a chance. "Do you know the Green Hotel?" She had printed out the page from the website and showed it to the Sikh.

"What is address?" He leaned in to look at it. "Ah. Near Chandni Chowk. Very good location. Near my Gurdwara. And Jama Masjid, very famous mosque. Yes, I can take you there. I know this place."

Relieved, Annie gave herself into his care. She settled into a wide back seat with torn leather cushions and no seat belts. Near the edge of the airport, he stopped and a second man got into the car. "My brother, I am just giving a lift to home," he explained. The two men chatted in Hindi the rest of the ride, which left Annie free to form powerful impressions of India's capital on the long and chaotic ride into the heart of the city.

It turned out the driver didn't actually know the place. By forceful stops and starts and vigorous horn work he made his way through a form of urban life Annie had never seen before, not even in movies. "This is Chandni Chowk, most famous street in Delhi!" the driver shouted. Even at this hour, the sidewalks and street edges were thronged with vendors, strollers, beggers, sleepers, tea stalls, vegetable sellers, cloth merchants, sick dogs, and rickshaws. Every foot of forward progress risked someone's life and limb. Overhead, dense tangles of electrical wires bought or stole power to businesses and residences in the large buildings nearly hidden from view by the life on the street.

They turned into a narrow lane with an iron fence down one side. Carts and bikes were tied to this fence, and in amongst them, whole families were bedded down to sleep on the asphalt. One young man was awake, leaning against the fence, a glow from the small *bidi* he was smoking. The driver rolled down his window and shouted, "*Bhai sahib, Green Hotel kahan hai?*" The bidi-smoker frowned, gazed around, waved his arms behind him, pointed up, and there was a large neon sign atop a building – 'Green Hotel' – that could be seen from a mile away but not from the nearest street.

The Green Hotel had a tiny but functional lobby, and an elevator to her third floor room. She would have liked a drink but the Green Hotel had no bar. Her room's central feature was a bed large enough to sleep a family of five. Its other feature was one straight-back chair. A tall window looked out into an empty gray space in the heart of the building and beneath it, an air conditioner rattled cold air into the room. The bathroom had a western-style toilet – thank God for that – with a faucet near the floor beside it. The shower was the whole room, with a showerhead protruding from the opposite wall. There was also a sink, with a drainpipe that stopped one inch from the floor drain. Altogether a depressing setting for the launch of her new life.

What have I done? she asked herself at three in the morning in this utterly foreign city. Less than a week ago she was a respectable and predictable wife, mother, and retired professional in the town where she had lived for thirty years. Her husband, whom everyone thought a decent man, may not have enjoyed her company, or respected her or treated her well, but in his own distorted way may have loved her. That was gone forever.

She opened her laptop, her only contact with any world she had known. The hotel's web page had promised free wi fi. She tried to get a signal, but there was nothing. So she opened her suitcase, pulled out a nightshirt, washed her face in cold water, and crawled into the family-size bed where she immediately fell asleep.

Annie stayed in Delhi only long enough to find a bookstore and get a train ticket to Dehra Dun. The May heat was unbearable; she could hardly breathe once she left the air conditioned Green Hotel. Mukesh, the morning desk clerk, was cheery and helpful:

"Madam, for books you must certainly visit the Delhi Bookstore in Darya Ganj. Very close to here. It has everything in science and computer."

"Can I walk from here?"

Mukesh took a step backward as if startled at the thought, and shook his head. "No, Madam, for such as yourself, it is not advisable."

"Also, I need to get a train ticket to Dehra Dun. How would I do that?"

"Madam!" he said, laying a hand on his chest. "You must leave that to me. You will find it very overwhelming to do this yourself."

"I'm sure you're right!"

"I will send my man. When does Madam wish to leave?"

"As soon as possible."

"I shall do my level best!"

At the Delhi Bookstore she bought a stack of books on programming, a couple of novels set in India, and a book on Hindu asceticism.

✲ ✲ ✲

Annie reached Rishkesh by the Hemkunt Express at 8 AM after a thirteen hour trip from Delhi. The hotel desk had purchased a sleeping berth for her. She arrived at the train station, found her train, her carriage, and discovered she would have four very intimate co-passengers in her compartment. Her luggage took up too much of the patch of footspace between facing seats, and she claimed a lower berth by putting her laptop bag on it. The upper berth was still folded tightly against the wall. By the time the train pulled out of Delhi, she was sharing this seat with a local couple who had two young children, all their luggage, and sacks with snacks and meals for the kids. When it came time for the upper berth to come down, the husband continued to sit on the lower berth beside Annie while his wife fussed with the children. With the berth down, there wasn't enough height to sit upright, so they sat hunched side by side, occasionally smiling at each other and trying to make polite conversation. This family went to Rishikesh every year in May to the holy places, they said, and to get away from the heat. Annie hoped that meant Rishikesh would be cool. Finally the family got itself settled, the two children on the upper berth opposite, and the husband climbed up to his upper bed over Annie, tossed a few times, and at last there was quiet and darkness as the train chugged northward to Rishikesh.

✲ ✲ ✲

CHAPTER 6

_____ ANTIQUITIES _____

The BMW was waiting for a passenger on the British Air flight from London, which arrived shortly after Annie's from Seattle. After a restful trip in first class, Nic Grayson made his way through the familiar hurdles at Indira Gandhi International Airport, exiting to meet the driver from the Maurya Hotel in the embassy district where he always stayed in Delhi.

Nic was in his late forties, a trim, savvy, and sophisticated traveler and businessman. He knew his way around, with the easy manners of privilege. At the Maurya, he greeted the desk clerk, whom he really did remember from his previous trips, with what seemed like warmth.

"Welcome back, sir. Mr. Dominic Grayson III?" Mr. Sanjay Mishra, said, reading from his computer screen. "Executive club suite? How many nights, sir?"

"Six days, but perhaps longer. Could you leave the numeral off? Not really necessary, is it?" He didn't know how this numeral kept turning up.

"No, sir. No numeral." With a deferential smile, Mishra made a note in the computer.

Nic's family went way back in India, at least six generations, to the time when a distant great-grandfather had come out to Calcutta in 1810 as a 'writer' for the East India Company. That ancestor had been known as simple Wm. Gray. That had been a good time to start out in India, when everything was still open and there were still undiscovered angles for getting rich. His great-great-great-grandfather had taken an interest in history and archaeology, making alliances with ambitious Brahmins and Kayasthas, the literate castes, who were willing to tie their family fortunes to the new British elite.

The angle Nic's ancestors had figured out was antiquities. Almost any bronze or stone carving could be sold in Europe, and any fresco that could be stripped off walls could go to museums, and they began collecting everything they could get their hands on. These were packed in crates and shipped home by the score. The family business was passed down, each generation richer than the last, and Nic was the latest heir. They knew everyone, they had agents all over India, and they were extremely rich. Even so, it was still a small hands-on business, which Nic closely supervised, because he liked the work.

In recent decades, the antiquities trade had gone underground with the passing of protective legislation by the Government of India, and Nic's family business, Indian Art and Antiquities [now renamed IndoArt International], had shifted to contemporary art, mostly paintings. This market was hot; modern Indian artists, many now living in London, were selling for millions. But many of the same buyers for a painting by Atul Dodiya or Tyeb Mehta asked about older works, sculptures from the 'tradition.' This was a more delicate and less public business. . . but business all the same.

Mr. Mishra handed Nic the key card and said, "Have a good evening, sir. Your luggage will be delivered."

✿　✿　✿

Nic slept until late in the morning, but was up, shaved, and dressed in time for a lunch meeting. He communicated with his New Delhi Agent, Seema Chakravarti, by email, and they had agreed to meet at 1:00 PM in the lobby. For an art dealer, the lobby of the Maurya, a cross between St. Paul's Cathedral and a Buddhist cave temple, was the best meeting place in Delhi, under the spectacular ceiling paintings.

Seema arrived on the dot, bubbling with delight to see Nic. "Nic darling, so good to see you!" She wore tight jeans and high heels, a loose white silk shirt, and strands of gold chains. Her arms jingled as she reached to give him an engaging embrace. "Good trip? Or not so good?" She checked his mood.

"Always so beautiful," he said in return, his hand stroking the silk for just a second. "Good enough, good enough." He gestured to the seat opposite him at the small table.

"Murderous hot!" she exclaimed, although she looked cool. Her hair was loosely pulled back in a thick bun, with strands artfully falling down the sides. "You're crazy to come this time of year. Why didn't we meet in London? I'd like that better."

"I believe it was you who said there were some interesting developments, sweetheart." For this kind of business, they didn't use email; it was always in person.

"Did I? Oh, I guess you're right." She laid a folder on the table between them, and patted it. "well, here it is. But tell me first, how is Claire?"

"Claire is home staying cool. She told me to go with her blessings."

"Hmmm," said Seema, tilting her head to look at him flirtatiously. "Well, that's something, Claire's blessings."

"I thought so."

He picked up the folder and flipped it open. There were a dozen or so sheets, poor computer copies of photographs. He looked at them without comment or expression. They were photographs of individual works of art, numerous washed out sandstone sculptures, pedestals, featureless Vishnus or Brahmas, hard to tell which, a couple of lingams, a Buddha with nose, ears, and arms knocked off. "Well," he said, noncommittally. He closed the folder and put it back on the table.

"These are from our Meerut friends," she said.

"Did I fly here for this?"

She gave him a teasing smile. "No, there's more. But no photo. We'll have to go for a ride."

☆   ☆   ☆

On the same day that Annie was finding a bookstore in Darya Ganj, Nic and Seema arrived by private car to a street near the Green Hotel and the Jama Masjid. The great mosque is surrounded by a warren of tiny streets filled with shops specializing in wedding paraphernalia, fancy invitations, grooms' ornaments, picture frames, photo albums, fireworks. In an obscure niche off the side of a side street they entered a photography shop where a young man sat watching television. He jumped up, promised to be right back, and soon returned with an older man, his uncle. They were ushered into a tiny ovenlike inner room where Uncle turned on an air conditioner. "Please, sit," he said, offering two chairs.

"Tell him about the Kamakhya Kali," Seema said.

✫ ✫ ✫

Mohan Ram began with the myth. Goddess Shakti in her form as Sati married Shiva without her father's permission. Her father was Himalaya, and he didn't want the rude yogi-god for a son-in-law. Himalaya decided to hold a *yagna*, a fire sacrifice, to which he invited all the gods except his son-in-law. Sati was furious at this insult, and decided to go anyway. In a rage, she threw her body into the sacrificial fire to pollute it, and was burned (although she herself left that body and took up as Parvati). Shiva was so grief-stricken that he picked up her body and began his mad tandava dance, threatening to dance til her body was decayed. The other gods feared that he would destroy the world before he was done, so Vishnu followed him around, cutting up Sati's body with his discus as they went. Pieces fell all over India, and wherever a body part landed, important temples grew up of the *shakt* variety, devoted to goddess worship. The most important part was her vulva, which landed in far off Assam, and the temple built over it is the Kamakhya Temple.

Nic listened to this story with his arms folded across his chest, nodding now and then, a bit of a smile playing on his lips. He had heard it many times before. He was waiting for the part about a sculpture he could get his hands on, how old it was, what its history was, what condition it was in.

Everyone knows the Kamakhya Temple is the most famous of the *shakti peeths*, Mohan Ram went on, the places of Devi's powerful body parts. Kamakhya is the most powerful place of all. And in the deepest part of that temple, there is not even an image of Devi. No; rather there is the mouth of a cave and a natural spring from which flows the fluids of Shakti. And for three days every summer, it flows red, as Shakti has her 'impure time,' Mohan Ram said delicately, which is the time of the great Ambuvaci festival.

"The opening to the cave and the spring is covered with a red sari," Seema added. "For modesty."

Yes, everyone knows about this cave, but what few people know is that once there was a Devi image in it. Mohan Ram stopped dramatically to let this sink in.

Nic bit. "When?"

"Long time past. We are not knowing exact date, but before Maharaja of Koch Bihar refused to worship there."

"When was that, approximately?" Nic had his limits. Of course, the whole thing would have to get researched, but he needed enough pegs in the ground to know whether he wanted to go on with this.

"It was rebuilt in 1665 after Muslims destroyed it," said Seema, who had done her research. "He is saying he's got something from the pre-Muslim period. That was probably Kalapahar who destroyed it in 1568. That's the latest it could be."

"So. An image that may have been in place where the cave with the spring is now. Let's hear about it. Describe it."

Small cups of chai arrived, sweet and hot. "This is very excellent murti, Sir. In very good condition. It is Kali in *pratyalidha* pose, four arms, standing on Lord Shiva. She holds sword and human head."

"How big?"

"Maybe four feet. I have not measured exactly. Very fine condition, nothing missing, except for a very small piece of the back part of the left leg, not even visible from the front. All arms, nose, fingers. . . ."

"Well, then, let's see it. Where is it?"

"Ah, sahib, that is problem."

Seema frowned. She had been under the impression that they had it in a crate in the back room. That was the point of bringing Nic all this way. "It's not here?"

"Not at this moment, sorry. You see. . . ," another long story began. "My uncle is the one who got it, from a priest in Gauhati. This is very old priest, very poor, very needy. My uncle saw it in small shrine in west of the town belonging to this priest. He saw it was in good condition and made in old style. He spent long time going back, going back, making friends with priest. Priest tell him all his problems, how much money he need. My uncle offer him that much money, plus that much again. Two times what that priest need. That priest say he cannot sell Mother; how he do that? My uncle say he build new temple for Ma Kali, so not to worry. Finally, priest take money, my uncle take Kaliji."

Nic and Seema waited for the other shoe to drop.

"My uncle bring to Banaras, where he have warehouse. So then I see."

"When did you see it?"

"I see last September at Durga Puja. My uncle take Kali Ma out for worship. Our family shakt, we worship goddess with goat every year at Durga Puja. This very great and ancient murti of Kali, we offer her goat at Durga Puja."

"And you were there."

"Yes! I was there, I see all! Priest come, cut throat, much blood, we eat *prasad* of goat."

Seema, a vegetarian from a Vaishnavite family, winced. Nic, a meat-eating Brit, also winced.

"Since then, family have very good fortune!" Mohan Ram laughed and spread his hands at all the good fortune – albeit invisible – that had come to his family along with Kali Ma. "And best fortune is give Kali Ma to you, sahib." The price had yet to be negotiated.

Mohan Ram's family was in the antiquities trade business, just like Nic was. Their part of the trade was finding objects in the villages and lost corners of cities where impoverished Hindus could be induced to part with their treasures in exchange for rupees. Nic's job was to provide believable provenance descriptions, get them past the customs bureaucracy, and to wealthy buyers abroad.

"Where is it now? Still in Banaras?"

"Now we come to problem, sir. When memsahib tell me you come, I go to Banaras to get Kali Ma. My uncle say, Kali Ma gone away. 'Where to?' I say. Never mind, he get it back."

"I paid a deposit on it," Seema reminded him. "You insisted on that."

Mohan Ram sighed. "Yes, I tell my uncle that. He say he get it back soon."

"Well, where is it? Maybe we can help?" This from Nic, leaning forward.

"I am not knowing. He would not say. He just say, 'I get it back, give me a little time.'"

"How much time?"

"A few weeks, sir."

It was agreed that Seema would keep in touch with Mohan Ram, who would put pressure on his uncle to retrieve the lost Kamakhya Kali. Nic would stay on for a couple of weeks, at least, because he had other business in Delhi. In the meantime, Seema would try to find out more about a here-to-fore unknown Devi image that once inhabited the Kamakhya temple. While she was working on that, Nic had schmoozing to do with the legitimate artists and collectors of the city.

CHAPTER 7

AUDIENCE WITH
THE SWAMI

S wami Shaktinanda held his morning audience on the roof of his three-story
ashram on the great upper curve of the Ganges where it sweeps out of the
Sivalik range and down onto the plains. Annie observed how everyone adored
this river, raising their hands in prayer to it each time they saw it. The river at
Rishikesh is fast-running and shallow, rushing along its gravelly bed as if in a
hurry to reach the great towns further south where the river goddess is worshipped
in great riverside temples and fed with the corpses of Hindu dead. In the early
morning, a light breeze drifts downriver and fans early risers with scents of deodar
and eucalyptus and alluvial dust.

Arriving at the Rishikesh station, Annie had found a noisy *vikram* to take her
upriver to the northern end of town where most of the ashrams were, including
Bhav Dham Ashram. This gave her a chance to get a good look at the brightly
painted temples and ashrams, the plaster statues of gods, and white- and orange-
robed *sadhus* and *sanyasis* lounging at river's edge. Many of them had their sect
marked on their foreheads, three horizontal streaks for worshippers of Shiva, two

vertical ones for Vishnu, or a red streak for Devi. Most were men, but there were occasional stooped and withered women, their long gray braids hanging down their saffron robes. Karen had told her about these women and their interesting lives, but they looked like holy bag ladies to Annie.

The swami sits on a platform under a thatched roof, the sun rising behind him. Around him, in cross-legged little groups blinking in the sun, are some of his many devotees, giddy with the thrill of being in his presence. The swami is felt to be ancient, and vibrant with divine insight, even though he is only a man in his forties. He is said to have been incarnated fourteen times in India since the battle of the Mahabharata, twelve times by birth, and twice by transferring his soul into another body. That is why his eyes are unlike other men's eyes; his devotees can feel his black pupils drill into them. They shiver with excitement at the thought that he can see right through their flesh and into their souls. Annie watched his eyes and tried to avoid them.

It was clear from the facial features of his devotees this bright May morning that they are from all over the world. They have brought gifts, simple things like bananas and oranges and boxes of sweets. They also have envelopes filled with cash, which they present along with the food offerings, handing them to Swamiji's assistant, a young man named Narayan who sits deferentially at his feet. From the back where Annie is sitting, uncomfortably cross-legged and feeling fraudulent, there appears to be some kind of dispute under discussion between the swami and a middle-aged Nepali couple at his feet. They have handed an envelope to Swamiji's assistant, Narayan, who reports its contents to the swami.

"Two life memberships are two thousand rupees each," the assistant explains. They seem to have thought it was two thousand per couple. "When will the balance be paid?" Annie cannot hear the reply, but the matter seems to get resolved. Swamiji then asks, "And how are your family?" There is a marriage issue for their daughter they wish to discuss with him, which goes on for some time. After a little while, a receipt is brought for the couple.

Annie is starting to worry about her lack of a gift. She isn't asking for a lifetime membership, so should she be offering money? Is a bunch of bananas good enough for her request for a room? She could offer a thousand rupees and let him determine how long she could stay for that amount.

"Does anyone else wish to talk to me?" the swami asks, smiling across the crowd. His drill-bit eyes search the gathering; Annie leans to her left to hide behind another devotee. His eye settles on a young woman who seems obviously European, dressed in a sari with the end pulled modestly over her blond hair. She shakes her head nervously. Narayan laughs and says, "Just here for *darshan*." She nods, blushing.

Narayan whispers to the swami, drawing his attention to a woman sitting beside her husband at the edge of the group near Annie. Annie had noticed her, too. She appeared disturbed, and seemed to be falling asleep frequently, then waking with a shudder. "Daughter," he says to her, inviting her to speak. Her husband answers for her.

"She has visions, Swamiji. She gets like this. . . ," he gestures toward her, "for long periods. Then she wakes and tells me what she sees." The small group around the swami is electrified by this information.

"Daughter," the swami says to the woman, "who do you see in your vision?"

The woman starts to sway and moan a little. "Ma! Ma!" she cries. There are gasps from the crowd. The swami sits up straighter, squints his eyes; Narayan asks, "Who are you, Mother?"

The woman continues to sway and moan. "Ma!"

"Speak, Mother," Narayan pleads. All eyes are fastened on this woman, who seems to be in a trance. After a few minutes her moaning turns into words, and people strain to understand, but it is neither Hindi nor Bengali. Someone recognizes the language: "Tamil." Her cries go on for several minutes, sending shivers down everyones' spines.

Swamiji begins to speak to the crowd over the moans of the woman. He says they have been seeing a great deal of this since the manifestations of a few months ago. Many, many have felt Her presence in astonishing ways. He himself has had visitations.

The young European woman in the sari begins to tremble. It seems to be catching. Narayan touches her arm, saying "Sister, what is it?" Her arm flails. Swamiji puts his hand on Narayan's arm and says, "Wait." The young woman calls: "Devi! Deviji!"

"Be calm, Daughter," Swamiji soothes her. "Where are you from?"

"Germany," she says. Her trembling subsides.

"Why have you come? What do you want?"

"I want to stay here and learn." She speaks very gently and shyly, her fragile demeanor creating an answering shift in the swami and in Narayan. Annie can tell she is quite young and rather attractive. Swamiji smiles.

"We can see you have a good spirit. Are you willing to work hard at your spiritual efforts?"

The German girl nods. Her eyes are shiny with adoration as she gazes at the swami. "We will help to show you the way." She begins to weep softly. "You may stay here with the other women. Can you do *jap?*" She nods.

"You must do one hundred and eight *om namah shivaya* each day. That is how to begin. Will you do this?" He drills her with his eyes. The German girl nods again, grateful for the beginning of instruction.

"Do you have *rudrakshamala*?"

She shakes her head. From an unseen stash behind Swamiji's chair, Narayan pulls out a rosary consisting of one hundred and eight rudraksha beads and presses it into her raised hands.

Swamiji turns back to his audience, gazing over the crowd, looking for someone else. "Don't look at me!" Annie thought, feeling like a third grader desperate not to be noticed.

"Who else has had a vision?" His eye settles on Annie. "I believe another has seen Devi." Narayan follows his gaze, and speaks directly to Annie.

"Answer, madam," he encourages. Annie hates being called madam, but was starting to get used to it. "Swamiji is asking."

"I believe you, too, have seen Her," Swamiji repeats. Annie feels his eyes. She has to say something. He seems certain of what she is going to reply, while Annie groped for something, anything, to say. She knew very well about herself that she was NOT a potential hypnotic subject, having washed out of a large scientific study of hypnotism as a graduate student at the university. They were looking for good subjects, and Annie was a failure from the first embarrassing attempt. She was way too skeptical.

"Tell us, Sister."

"I'm. . . um. . .I'm not sure."

The crowd was taking a keen interest in this next manifestation. She felt all their eyes and hearts hoping for more evidence of Swamiji's power.

"Tell us what you saw," Narayan said encouragingly.

Annie was desperate. "Well, um. It was late at night. I couldn't sleep. . . I got out of bed. I saw a woman dressed in a blue robe. . . ." She couldn't believe the words coming out of her mouth. She omitted some details, like turning on the computer.

"What did she look like?"

"She had blonde hair. And a very slim waist. She was young and beautiful." Someone in the audience sighed. "And long ears."

"How many arms did she have?" Narayan asked. Clearly the audience thought this was an interesting question. All heads turned back to her.

"Two." There seemed to be some disappointment. "And she had very powerful weapons."

"Weapons!" Narayan repeated, with interest. "What kind of weapons?"

"Well, she had a fireball she could roll in her hands and toss a great distance at her enemies."

"She was fighting enemies?"

"Yes, she hurled her fireball at them, and they would fall down dead. She also had a frostbolt. And a wand. I saw her kill many fierce enemies." The audience waited for more as Annie tried to think of details to support her really outrageous story. "In my vision I was instructing her. She was a mage, and I was telling her who to kill. It was like it was me, but also someone else. This mage was me," she added.

A total silence fell on the audience, on Narayan, and on Swamiji. Annie could hear the rushing of the Ganges far below, and crows screaming over the hills. She had strained credulity, gone way overboard, they had seen right through her, she was going to be evicted.

Finally, Narayan spoke: "Madam, is it your wish to stay here for a while?"

"Yes. That is why I have come."

Narayan glanced at Swamiji, who nodded. "You may stay. You are welcome."

The building where the female renunciants stay was on a rise facing a broad courtyard and the river beyond. It consisted of a dozen narrow rooms connected by a fronting screened verandah. Annie's room contained a cot, an armchair, and a small table, all that a person needs except for a bathroom, which was at the far end of the building. A single shelf was set into the brick wall, where Annie lined up her books. She laid out her laptop on the table and opened it, hoping against hope for an internet connection, but there was nothing. She was going to have to be self-contained for the duration. She hoped she was going to be able to work on her computer textbooks while she was here, but there was going to be quite a lot of *satsang* and meditation and other religious activities.

"Welcome," said a merry voice from the doorway. An elderly, sweet-faced woman seemed genuinely delighted to see Annie. "I'm your next door neighbor. My name is Tyagi Ma." She said this in perfect though accented English. "Where are you from? Are you English?"

"American."

"Ah. I am Tamil, from Madras. I hope you can understand my English."

"Perfectly! I'm thrilled to have someone I can talk to. Not much Hindi, I'm afraid."

"Oh, no need for Hindi here. But down there. . ." she pointed toward Rishikesh town, ". . . it comes in handy. May I ask how long you will stay?"

"I don't know. A while, at least. I am taking it one step at a time." That was all Annie could truthfully say.

"That is EXACTLY how to proceed! You are quite right." Tyagi Ma smiled approvingly at Annie. "And you are going to need to buy yourself some new clothing." Tyagi Ma was dressed in a saffron sari, tightly wrapped, with its tail end tucked compactly at her waist. "You should get a white sari, or else salwar-kameez. That's much more comfortable. That is correct clothing for novices." Annie was already feeling inappropriate in the loose pants and bright green silk kurta she had bought in Delhi. It made a loud statement in a world of ashramite understatement.

"Yes, I'll do that right away. And how long are you staying?" Annie seemed to understand she was at some kind of retreat such as the Catholic priory ran in her town, where people came for the weekend to get a dose of spiritual medicine from the sisters.

"I have been here fourteen years now."

"Fourteen years! That's a long time."

"Yes!" Tyagi Ma giggled girlishly. "I first came here twenty years ago. I had two friends who were older than me, and we went on a pilgrimage to Gangotri. We had heard of this ashram and its famous swami, the one before this one. Visitors were welcome and we came and stayed three or four days before we went back to Madras. That was how I knew I wanted to come to this place. It was a very male place then."

"There are more women now?"

"SO many more women! When I first came here, I did not see any. But lately, so many women have taken these vows."

"Why is that? Why do they want to come here?"

"I think I can explain it." Tyagi Ma took a step closer to Annie, and asked: "Do you know about Gargi?"

"Gargi? No."

"She was the eldest wife of Yajnavalkya in ancient times. Yajnavalkya decided to renounce – do you know *sanyas?* – yes, he was going to renounce, and so he divided his wealth between his two wives. And the younger wife was happy to take the property and stay back, but Gargi said, 'I don't want your money or your property. I too want freedom, liberation. And she also left home.' So it is now for many women. They want liberation."

"Yes, it's what many women want," mused Annie, thinking about the home and husband she herself had just renounced. "But what are they after? Just to live in freedom? Or, is it. . . what is it called. . . *moksha?*"

Tyagi Ma laughed. "Oh, no, I don't want moksha. My goal is, uh, to tell you the truth, I believe in the guru, Shaktinandan. We all live in darkness, and what is God? It is very hard to know God. But we can know the guru. He has been there, he knows the path, he will guide us. Have you had *darshan* of Swamiji? Oh, you must have, or you wouldn't be here."

"Yes. This morning. He gave me permission to stay here. He is quite amazing. His eyes. . . ."

"Oh, yes!" she sighed. "You can just feel his power!" She gave a little shiver. "Yes, I follow Swami Shaktinandan. Here we all follow him."

"Are there many others? Young women, too?"

"More and more. Some of these young women have great spiritual powers. Through the help of Swamiji they are brought close to the divine Mother, the Maha Shakti. Some now are very advanced." Tyagi Ma's voice dropped. "There have been many startling things recently. I could tell you such things!" She leaned out of the doorway where she was standing to check both directions down the verandah.

"Please do tell me! I am very interested in this."

"But later. We have *satsang* now. Have you been, or is this your first?"

"My first."

"Then let's go together!"

Annie was again feeling severely fraudulent as she sat among a hundred or more women and men in the large meditation hall, men on one side, women on the other. Never in her life had she dreamed of getting involved in Hindu worship. She knew about the stream of Americans who came to India to drop out or get high or get spiritual during the sixties, including most famously of all, the Beatles. Who had actually come to Rishikesh! The Hare Krishnas, on the other hand, mostly annoyed her when she saw them dancing on street corners. She had read *Siddhartha* as an undergrad in the sixties, and it had appealed to her, of course, as it did to everyone who read it, but she never imagined that sixth century BC India of the novel would be what she'd find in India today. She was *interested* in all this, but never for any personal religious reasons, of which she had lost pretty much the whole impulse around the age of twenty. Now here she was, sitting stiffly cross-legged as the women around her sang blissful *bhajans* with their eyes closed. Annie felt not only fraudulent, but ashamed of her cynicism.

Words of wisdom were inscribed along the wall. "God has given you two ears and two eyes but only one tongue, so that you should see and hear more than you speak."

"The individual soul is filled with impurities and blinded by worldly distractions."

"All life is of God and God is in all life."

She did find these inspirational.

Since the hymns were in Hindi, Annie couldn't sing along, so she just sat still, hands in her lap, eyes shut. She spent the time working out how she would go about discovering who or where Shobha was. Chances were good that she was sitting right here in this room, but Karen hadn't been able to provide a photo of her. If Annie were to directly ask Tyagi Ma about Shobha, she would probably get a quick answer, but something held her back. For one thing, once she turned over the stone she had no further reason to stay on, and the problem with that was she had no further destination. The meaning of her life, for now, was that stone and meeting Shobha. Maybe she didn't want to exhaust that meaning too quickly. So Annie felt she should observe the one-tongue principle: look and listen with her two eyes and two ears, and spare the tongue. Besides, if there were some kind of intrigue around the stone and Shobha's ownership of it, the sudden appearance of a foreigner asking about Shobha might complicate whatever else was going on.

After satsang there was a meal, and Annie was starving. Tyagi Ma led the way to another courtyard that was shaded by an enormous peepul tree. It sat a foot higher than the courtyard and was surrounded by a low stone ledge where many elderly orange-robed men were sitting with their trays of food. The heat was oppressive and the stone ledge looked inviting, since it was the only place to sit and the only shade, but no women would get a place there. Mats had been spread beside a wall where there was a bit of shadow, and this was for the women. Across the courtyard women were lining up to receive a tin plate; they moved from pot to pot and were served rice, dal, vegetables, and yogurt. Tyagi Ma and Annie took a seat on one of the mats and went to work. Annie waited to watch Tyagi Ma create a little ball of rice, dip it into the dal, and pop it into her mouth. Annie copied her, as best she could. After dinner, Tyagi Ma showed her how to clean her own plate and cup, and stack them on a rack to dry.

In this way, life seemed about to settle into a routine. Astonishingly, it was exactly ten days since Annie had walked out of the house on Junot Street. She thought of another aphorism to put on the wall of the meditation house:

"It is possible to leave one life and begin another in ten days. Just do it."

Chapter 8

BANARAS

S eema met Nic deep in the underground of the Maurya Hotel where there was a replica of a London pub one night a week later. Nic was drinking Harp beer because he was surprised to see it on the list. Seema ordered iced tea.

"News," she said, sitting down with her usual jingle of gold. "My sources tell me there have always been rumors of an actual murti at Kamakhya. For instance, there's a reference to it in an 1825 letter from a Krishan Das to a John Gray. . . , " here she paused to point at Nic across the table with a laugh, "an ancestor of yours, I think! – about a black marble Kali rescued from the Kamakhya temple and hidden by Brahmins."

"How did we let that one slip away?" he asked. He was sitting with his arm thrown across the back of the booth, finally relaxed and more to the point, cool after a day of fighting through the heat from gallery to studio, meeting with owners of several of Delhi's oldest art venues. He was also negotiating with a new talent to take a dozen of her best works to London to show in his new South Bank gallery. Now he enjoyed watching Seema, as well as listening to her. She was one of the reasons he came personally to Delhi about these acquisitions rather than sending an assistant.

"Apparently he almost got his hands on it. He had planned on including it in the crate heading to London, but the letter explained that the Brahmin family had disagreed on whether to sell it. He was optimistic that he'd be sending it with his next shipment." Seema's iced tea arrived.

"Well that's interesting. Builds a story for the image. Always improves the price."

"After that, the trail grows cold. Unless there's more correspondance about it in your family archives in London."

"I'll have someone look into that." He chugged his beer.

A group of Australians at a nearby table were getting raucous, with many open glances at Seema, who was the only woman in the pub.

"We could go somewhere more private," Nic said.

"Where would that be?" She arched her eyebrows.

"Why not upstairs?"

"Why not?"

Later, lying nude in the sumptuous sheets and duvets of Nic's room, Seema asked about Nic's two children, Isabella and William. Nic reached for his wallet on the side table and pulled out a photo, bent to the shape of his wallet, which was bent to the shape of his own rear end. A blonde five year old in a polka dot one piece swimsuit, was romping in a back yard pool. A three-year old toddler was manning the hose.

"Ah, they are adorable!" Seema cooed. It was these youngsters who made Seema's situation so hopeless.

"That was last summer. They're bigger now, of course."

"Of course. They both look like you." She had never seen a photo of Claire, and she never wanted to, so it was only a guess. Nic gave Seema an affectionate kiss on the cheek for her effort. He tucked the photo back into his wallet, and turned back to Seema with renewed intentions.

"I have you now. Let's focus on now."

"Always only these little 'nows,'" she pouted. "Okay, I'll take what I can get." She turned to him with intensity.

Their affair began three years earlier, when Nic was in Delhi to inspect what was reported to be three letters written from prison by Nehru to his daughter, Indira, in 1934. Nic needed someone to verify their authenticity. He was directed to the Nehru Memorial Museum and Library where a young assistant to the director, the beautiful Seema, agreed to take a look at them. With only a brief look, she thought they were probably authentic; she worked with the archival materials in the museum, and the handwriting and the paper seemed like everything else she was familiar with. Of course there were additional tests that could be run. Most importantly, the content was new; these were previously unknown letters. The only problem was that if they were authentic, they belonged in the library and she felt obliged to try to acquire them rather than see Nic take them off to sell to a rich collector. This led to a running debate that required many lunches in interesting settings, and wasn't resolved until one afternoon in which six yards of aqua silk were strewn on the floor of Nic's hotel room and Seema yielded unconditionally. Shortly after that negotiating triumph, she came to work for Nic.

Nic had sold the letters to a rich collector, who then donated them to the museum, so everything worked out for the best, as Nic liked to remind her. As for subsequent purchases, there were always workable rationales. An article was taken from careless obscurity to worldwide esteem. Or, his acquisition, which required careful researching of its pedigree, added to the sum of human knowledge and the brilliance of the object itself, which took on new life. Money was not always evil; in fact, it did a great deal of good in the world. People needed more of it, not less. The trade in art and antiquities added new strands of wealth in the world economy, that allowed the surpluses of billionaire collectors to trickle down to people like Mohan Ram. Or even that poor priest in Gauhati.

After a second round of love-making, Seema was back to thinking about the Kamakhya Kali. Her own cascade of black hair was strewn across the pillows, and her sexuality had knocked Nic as flat as Shiva under Kali's feet. "Just think of the history of KK," she said.

"KK?" he murmured, half asleep.

"Kamakhya Kali."

"Ah. Right."

"Carved by some unknown carver maybe six hundred years ago. Lives a century or two in a musty cave with a natural spring under a temple. When conquerors come, intent on destroying the likes of her, she is spirited away by Brahmins. Who knows where they keep her, until it is safe to bring her out again? But why not put her back in the original temple?"

"Because no one remembers that's where she came from." Nic is still half asleep, but he's listening.

"Right. All they know is they have a beautiful murti. Maybe they've been secretly worshipping it all along, like in a household shrine. Or maybe it was in storage. But eventually it ends up in the little neighborhood temple in Gauhati that Mohan Ram described."

Seema lay looking at the ceiling, listening to Nic breathing. He had fallen asleep again.

"But how do WE know that's where it came from? Don't we have a missing link? Is the reference to Kamakhya Temple in the letter to John Gray in 1925 evidence enough?" She looked at Nic, who was fast asleep. This was her job, not his. He would take her evidence, and her story, and attach it to the object when he sold it. "And, of course, where is it now?"

She stroked Nic's smooth chest thoughtfully, then kissed his shoulder. "We not only have a missing link, we also have a missing goddess."

Seema decided she needed to go to two places: to Banaras, to see Mohan Ram's uncle, and to Gauhati, to find the priest who gave KK up. One thing she badly needed was a photo. She had only verbal descriptions to go on, and while they were intriguing, she needed some visual evidence that she wasn't being scammed. Even with visual evidence, it might be a scam.

After showering and dressing and pinning order back into her hair, she said to Nic, who was putting on socks and shoes, using a chair as a footstool, "Come with me to Banaras."

"Are you kidding? In May?"

"It's hotter right here in Delhi."

"Right. But here we've got the Maurya. Also, I've got work to do here. You go, Sweetheart. Tell me all about it afterward."

She wanted him to go with her. On the other hand, she had relatives in Banaras, and it might be more discreet to stay with them, like a modest young Indian woman, than in a hotel with Nic. Banaras could be a small town.

"Okay. But promise after that, you'll go with me to Gauhati."

Nic put his foot down and stood up. "Gauhati? Hmm. That might interest me."

"Okay? It's a deal?" She tipped her head flirtatiously. He kissed her.

"Okay. Deal."

The Chakravartis had a large residence near Banaras Hindu University, a big house filled with many Chakravartis of all ages. The patriarch was her father's uncle, a distinguished professor of geology at the university. He was a benevolent despot over a household filled with several sons, their wives, and children. Despite the definite patriarchal authority of the household, it always felt to Seema like a women's hostel, filled with chattering females of all ages, including charming little toddling ones, whereas the men were generally elsewhere. She loved coming here, to be embraced by their warm world and even their invasive questions. And then she loved to escape to her freedom in Delhi. In between times, it was a tussle to defend her unmarried status and everyone's alarm about her unsettled future. But her sophistication armored her against their strongest admonitions, because they all saw her as a New Woman, unlike them, and who knows, such women – independent, with careers rather than husbands – might not be a totally bad option in the India of the future. That's how liberal this family was.

So Seema found herself once again surrounded by her female relatives, all asking questions and giggling and telling their own stories. Two tykes, ages three and four, tried to show her their toys, while two large-eyed teenage girls questioned her about her life in Delhi. There was also the shy new bride of her youngest male cousin, sitting quietly but watching intently. When Seema asked to see the photo album of her wedding the previous year, she was happy to produce it. She sat by Seema and they leafed through it, identifying everyone.

"Here you are, Seema," said four year old Chinu, pointing to Seema mugging with a group of cousins.

"Yes, that's me! And here's you!" Little Chinu leaned in to look closely, then looked up at Seema with a big grin.

Interrogated about the purpose of her trip to Banaras, Seema revealed that she had to meet with an art vendor on behalf of her boss.

"Rakesh will accompany you," insisted Kakiji, her aunt. Seema protested that there was no need, but she knew it was hopeless. This family would never consent to her roaming around Banaras alone. Rakesh would come with her; there would be no way out of this male protection.

CHAPTER 9

FOUR FRIENDS

There is an iron gate on the back side of the ashram that leads to a little-used road behind the fringe of temples and ashrams that line the river. The uphill side of the road is mostly the kind of scrub forest that covers the lower Himalaya range and gives shelter to a myriad of creatures who live protected lives in Rishikesh's *ahimsa* environs. This road is beloved of the patrons of the ashrams, who use it as a contemplative trail for morning and afternoon meditations in nature. They also use it as a private route to town. Now and then a noisy three-wheeled vikram putters up it, carrying an elderly renunciant back to her ashram, or a forest service jeep comes rumbling down from forest roads further uphill, but it is mostly as serene as the forest itself.

On a morning soon after Annie's arrival, four young renunciants, dressed in the white robes of novices, were strolling down this road, giggling and chattering with the carefree hearts of the unmarried girls they were. Because they were aimless, they weren't walking fast, which is the reason Annie, who had left the ashram behind them, soon caught up with them. She had her laptop tucked into a cloth shoulderbag, and she was not aimless. She was on her way to town in search of an internet connection.

"Hello!" they chorused as they turn to see Annie coming up behind them. "We know you. You are from our place, no?" said the one called Gitanjali.

"Yes! Hello. I am Annie."

"We know you are Annie," Gitanjali giggled. They all had roughly the same black braid down their backs, the same sweet, scrubbed faces, but Gitanjali seemed to be the most outspoken. She was not beautiful, but had a frank face and manner that invited trust.

"Do you know everything that goes on in the ashram?" Annie joked.

"yes. . . ," Gitanjali said.

"We try to. . . ," added Kunjlata.

"Where are you going?" they wanted to know.

"To town. Where are you going?"

"We are going to Triveni Ghat. You should come with us."

"Very holy place!" This was from Jaswanti, the most beautiful of the four. "You will like it. Please come." Jaswanti had lovely thick straight brows that sheltered deep-set eyes. She spoke with an earnestness that made you want to do as she asked.

Annie decided to take this opportunity to get to know these adorable girls who for some reason had renounced life at the very point of engaging it. Although in truth, they didn't seem very withdrawn at the moment.

Along the way they explained that Triveni Ghat was the confluence of three rivers, one of which was invisible. It was interesting to visit at this time of day because wandering sadhus and sanyasis from all over India come here in the summer. You could hear every language, see every act of devotion.

"Some are a little crazy," Gitanjali said, spinning her finger at her head, the universal sign. "Some are frauds."

"MANY are frauds," Sharada corrected. "They just want their free rice and free coins."

Annie wondered why these lovely young women were here, rather than at home with husbands and children. Of course, she herself was not at home with husband and children, but why weren't they? She asked them how they came to renounce.

"Gitanjali can tell you. She came first."

"Yes, Annie, you see, it was like this. When I was young I was very interested in kirtan and bhajans, religious stories and songs. My family was very devout. It was a good home to become a God-seeking person. I worshipped God, I read Gita. Our family Guru showed me the way. He gave me many books to read. The world is false and human birth is to reach God. At first I thought I could reach God at home. But there were many brothers and sisters in our house and I could not find solitude. So where could I go?"

Gitanjali had stopped along the road and was telling Annie this with all the passion of a medieval nun. This could be Hildegard of Bingen.

"When I was twenty-two my marriage was fixed. He was an engineer-lecturer. I tried to tell my parents that I did not want to marry. I am not liking this! But they did not listen. They fixed the date and I could not stop them. Finally only three days were left before my marriage and I was desperate. I left the house giving the excuse that I had to deliver an invitation to my friend's house, but instead I took a train to Vrindavan, the only place I knew to go. After I got there, I posted a letter to my father, but he did not get it. I stayed at an ashram for women there for a whole year. One day I posted a letter to my friend, and my father's brother intercepted it, so that's how they found out where I had gone. My parents came to get me. They promised if I would go back I could spend all my days at worship at home, but I would not go back. I was happy where I was."

"They didn't try to force you to go back?"

"No." Gitanjali shook her head. "They saw it would be useless. And besides that, the scandal of running from my marriage would make it impossible."

"Why is marrying such a bad thing? Wouldn't you come to love this engineer?"

"That is what my parents said. I didn't like the looks of the engineer. We met once, and I thought he would not come to love me, nor I him. And also, I thought, if I would marry I would not be happy but I would have to keep everyone else at home happy. And living among so many people and having so much work to do, I would not be able to spend a *sadhana* life. This is better."

"And Annie, you talk to the older women. You talk to Bramananda Mata. She always says, 'family life is NARAK!' Hell!" Kunjlata did such a good imitation that she made everyone laugh. "NARAK!"

As Annie kept asking them about their lives as renunciants, she found that they were all from the same town, and had run away one after the other, fleeing arranged marriages, to meet at Vrindavan, the birthplace of Krishna and a town kind to women renouncers and widows. From there they visited the sacred sites in Rishikesh and further up in the summer pilgrimage sites in the mountains. They had met the Swami, whom they called Gurudev, their "guru-god," on one of their stopovers, and been drawn to him. He invited them to settle in his ashram.

At the end of this story, there was a little flurry of whispered consultations. Annie gathered that they were trying to decide whether they could ask about something they were wondering about.

"Annie, may I ask you a question?" Kunjlata finally asked.

"Sure. What?"

"What is a mage?" Eight eyes watched her with anticipation.

Annie caught her breath.

"Is it like a magician?" Jaswanti wondered.

"They are saying you are a mage. But we don't know what that is," Gitanjali confessed.

Annie hesitated, searching for an answer.

"If you don't want to tell us. . . ."

"No, no. I will tell you. Although it is a little hard to explain. A mage is a kind of, a kind of warrior. . . who fights against evil."

They had stopped in the road again, the five of them in a little circle, frowns of perplexity on every single face.

"What kind of evil?"

"Well. . . as you know, there are many kinds." Annie looked at the forest. "Like in there, creatures that are dangerous." All eyes turned to peer into the brittle underbrush.

'Ah!" Gitanjali nodded; she understood. "There are wild boar in there. Very dangerous. Are you a hunter?" This would be simpler.

"No, not a hunter. There are worse kinds of evil." Annie searched for a story that would not be a lie. "There are people who do evil things. Evil people, actually. Mean people. Mages don't put up with it. They try to do something about it." Her story began to make sense to herself as it unfolded. "There are people with power over other people who make their life miserable and force them to do what makes them unhappy. Maybe they make that person feel stupid and unable to live up to their best. A mage will try to stop that." Four heads were nodding. They were familiar with this kind of evil.

"But how can she?"

"Does she have magical powers?"

"Well, yes, mages have great magical powers." Here Annie was entering uncertain territory, but she plunged forward. How to put this, without lying? "A mage has spells and powers to use against evil. She can use natural forces, like fire and ice. They say she can transport herself to here and there." She hoped never to be asked to demonstrate these powers.

Gitanjali and Kunjlata and Jaswanti and Sharada exchanged glances. "This sounds like Kaliji. Or Durga." They looked back at Annie with respect and awe.

As they continued on their way into town, Annie thought over her words. "I never said I was a mage," she told herself. But clearly a reputation of some kind was circulating in the ashram.

✿   ✿   ✿

Triveni Ghat was a seemingly endless stretch of concrete stairs leading down to the stony bank of the river at a wide spot where it divides into two channels before reuniting further downstream. It was another hot, hot day, long before the monsoons would reach as far west and north as Rishikesh, and the worshipful wading into the river that everyone was doing made absolutely good sense. People splashed right into the river in whatever they had on: saris, dhotis, trousers, loincloths, ochre robes. Women shampooed their hair, then changed from one sari into another without exposing more than a roll of stomach fat. Brahmins wearing sacred threads carried brass jars to offer *gangajal* to the sun. A few enormous trees offered shade back on the bank, beneath which you could buy the things needed to worship the river. There were little boats made out of leaves, chains of marigolds, incense, and camphor. Women and children were launching these little boats with tiny cargoes of flowers and camphor flame into the river. Smaller children splashed and romped and cooled off.

The four sisters and Annie waded in along with everyone else, laughing and splashing water onto their arms and heads. This was so inviting that they pushed further in, their robes drifting above their legs. Soon they were merrily splashing like the kids.

"Are you cooler now, Annie?" Kunjlata said as they walked dripping toward the shade of a banyan tree, carrying their sandals.

"You were looking too hot!"

"I WAS too hot!"

Near where they sat on a sparse bit of grass was a small temple with a tiny courtyard circled by an iron fence. Its gate opened and a woman in a white sari splashed a bucket of water over the courtyard. She began sweeping the debris from the night before out the front.

"Annie, that thing you said about mages transporting themselves here and there?"

"Yes?"

"That has been happening in our ashram."

"Really?" This drew Annie's attention from the clean-up in the little temple.

"Yes. Our Gurudev has been in three places at once."

They waited for Annie's response. All she could think of to say was, "Really? Tell me more."

"He was in satsang at our place. And a call came from Banaras, and they said he was there, giving a sermon. And then a call came from Kamakhya, and he was also there."

Annie examined their faces, wondering if they believed this. It was clear they did. "Wow. That is amazing." What else could she say? The skeptic in her was running through scenarios about how that could happen. A line of elderly emaciated sadhus was forming at the little temple, each carrying a little tin can with a handle.

"And another one. . . One of our *guru-behen*. . . ."

"Our sister with same guru. . . ."

". . . was here, meditating with Gurudev, then she flew to Kamakhya. . . ."

"NOT in a plane. . . ."

"No, like the mage, she was in Kamakhya, but also the same night I saw her with my own eyes on the very road we just came down!"

They had Annie's full attention now. "Who was. . . .This was one of your sisters?"

"Guru-behen. Yes, Shobha. And she is still in Kamakhya."

"She was getting power from many *tapas*."

Annie tried not to show too much astonishment – as a mage, this all should come as no surprise – but also because she did not want to reveal her prior interest in Shobha.

"How was she getting these powers?"

"From tapas. Doing many, many meditations. When you sit in meditation your concentration is toward God. You begin to feel God directly. You might start to get a few powers, God's power flows into you. But the danger is that your ego opens up and interferes. So you must be careful."

"Do you think Shobha was not careful?"

"We don't know. We don't know what happened to Shobha."

The line at the temple began to move slowly, as the sadhus received their portions of rice and dal and left to eat in privacy along the riverbank. The young women remembered it was almost time for satsang and they could not be late. Annie was no longer thinking about the internet; filled with curiosity and renewed motivation to find Shobha, she joined them for the long walk back.

At Satsang that night, there was a curious intensity of devotion and bliss. Swamiji did not always come to satsang, but he came in tonight, taking his seat on a throne in front of the deities, folding himself into a yogic pose, and closing his eyes into slits. Annie was close enough to him to see that his eyeballs were moving. He must be watching the devotees, or someone in particular.

Among the deities in the raised shrine were photographs of recent gurus, of several famous woman saints – Anandamayi Ma and Sharada – a pot-bellied Ganesh, a painting of Krishna and Radha snuggling in rapture. The principal deity, however, was a resplendent Kali in full vigor, blue-black, her left foot on Shiva, lying prone beneath her. This Kali was beautiful despite her gory ornaments of skulls and severed arms. She was recessed into another inner shrine that elevated her above the other deities and above Swamiji, where her face was shadowed by the red silk-hung overhang while low-wattage spotlights from behind gave her whole body an ethereal glow.

Little Tyagi Ma bustled around behind Swamiji, laying flowers in little plates in front of each of the secondary deities and adjusting the garlands on the images of Anandamayi Ma and Sharada.

Annie tried Swamiji's same trick, half-closing her eyes while scanning the devotees, at least the ones she could see without turning her head. The German girl was there, close to the front. The four friends from earlier in the day were also nearby. Jaswanti, the beautiful shy one, seemed totally blissed out, Annie thought. Is she in a trance?

The overhead lights had been dimmed to set a reverential mood, and therefore the fans, on the same dimmer switch, turned more slowly, so that the room on a hot May night was warming beyond endurance. The speaker system was producing a monotonous hymn-chant glorifying Devi, which the devotees were singing or humming along with. Annie was feeling faint from the heat and the sickening sweet smell of incense.

There was a sudden commotion near Annie; someone had fallen over. It was really too hot! Looking around, she saw it was Jaswanti, who had tipped back, falling into the lap of someone behind her. Her sisters had turned to her in alarm, but Jaswanti began calling, "Ma! Ma! Ma!" Annie couldn't be sure whether she was calling for her mother, as people do during stress, or was calling on the Goddess.

On his throne, Swamiji didn't budge. Narayan was no longer at his side, but Tyagi Ma had turned to look at the commotion. Then suddenly the lights in the whole hall went out, plunging the room into complete darkness. There were gasps of surprise, as devotees responded in different ways, some calling out in alarm, others urging calm until the power came back on. "It's okay, it's okay," said someone behind Annie. People were not too alarmed, since power outages were not unusual in Rishikesh. After a few moments, a few flashlights came on, including the one Annie always carried at night. These flickered around the room, trying to focus on the centers of commotion.

Annie's flashlight, which she had purchased at an airport shop in Frankfort, had a particularly strong beam, and because she felt she was suffocating on the floor, she stood up, and tried to direct her beam where it would be most helpful. Was that on Jaswanti, still passed out and calling for Ma, or on Swamiji, who presumably would give comfort to everyone? The beam circled the dais and shrine, lighting each of the figures wildly until finally coming to rest on Swamiji. He had turned to look at Kali and was just turning back toward the devotees as the beam found him and rested there. As he felt himself spotlighted, his face turned beatific, shining with the perspiration that everyone was experiencing, but in a way that seemed almost a halo around his head. Those who saw it remarked upon it later, how holy he had looked, how filled with divinity, under the mysterious beam of light.

And then the house lights returned, and the overhead fans picked up, and people said, "Thank you, Mother!" and "Jai Mataji!" There was a general settling down, as people returned to their meditation postures and took up heavy fanning with their little palm-frond fans. Annie had clicked off her flashlight and was just about to sit when there was a shriek from someone close to Swamiji.

The German girl was pointing to the murti of Kali. Everyone, including Annie, strained to look. Something was trickling down Kali's face, across her forehead, down her left eye. It pooled briefly in her eye socket before slowly dripping onto her cheek, where the light caught it brightly.

"Blood!"

"*Rakt!*"

People began standing again, leaning forward to get a better look. Already so close to the front, Annie was shoved closer, and when she understood what people were clamoring about, she turned her flashlight back on and aimed it at the Goddess's face. It was definitely blood.

"Oh my God," she muttered, stumbling as she was shoved from behind. Feeling the danger of a crush, she looked for an exit, or even a way to get against a side wall. In the jostle, her flashlight beam fell again on the swami.

Swamiji had stood and faced Kali. He raised his arms in praise, and then knelt in full *pranam* before the deity, and everyone took this as proof that this was truly a manifestation of Kali's presence. Others in front saw him, and did the same. As Annie stood in astonished silence, the entire audience dropped to their knees before this awesome manifestation of the Maha Shakti. Finally realizing she was the only one still standing, she flicked off her flashlight and sat down.

CHAPTER 10

MOHAN RAM'S UNCLE

S eema and Rakesh found the workshop in a warren of little streets behind the famous cremation ground of Manikarnika Ghat. Seema really hated this part of the city and the gruesome scenes at river's edge, with its constant stream of orange-shrouded corpses, which was particularly bad in May, when so many elderly people died from the heat. The smell of woodsmoke always made her shiver, as it connoted only cremation fires; it was the smell of death. It was unlucky to come upon these corpses being rushed through the streets, and even a few streets away, where she and Rakesh were searching for shop numbers, she could hear the drumming and shouting.

They had come to an unimpressive doorway with a grandiose sign: Lal Ram Import Export Emporium. In the small front showroom, one of the uncles stood behind a wide counter on which silk saris could be unrolled for the rare shopper who was dragged in off the tourist route. Through a narrow doorway off to the side, they came into a large storeroom filled with dusty counters covered in wooden carvings and silver jewelry, and stacked with crates. The room smelled of chana masala, which Mohan Ram and his uncle were eating from brown wrapping paper behind the counter. Mohan Ram jumped up, wiping his hands on a dusting cloth.

"Welcome, welcome," he gushed, embarrassed to have been caught in the act of eating.

"Please, finish," Seema said pleasantly. "I'll just look around."

"No, not at all, just finished now!"

Seema had called Mohan Ram at his office near Jama Masjid in Delhi for directions to the family warehouse in Banaras, and Mohan Ram had got on the next train in order to be here when she arrived by air. She wasn't exactly glad to see him. He namaste'ed elaborately to her and to Rakesh, his expression wondering who the young man was.

"My nephew, Rakesh," was all she said. Rakesh was nineteen years old, a student in commerce at Delhi School of Economics. He adored his Auntie Seema, who was only a few years older than he, and envied her job working for Nic's London-based company, hoping she would find a way to get him into it when he finished his degree. He looked around the warehouse appraisingly.

"My uncle, Lal Ram," Mohan Ram said, with a deferential wave toward his uncle.

Lal Ram was an even bigger man than Mohan Ram, with a broader bald head and a wider belly, but there was a clear family resemblance. He came forward gregariously with a namaste. This young woman was one of their most important clients, their pipeline to the lucrative antiquities market for high-end acquisitions. The small pieces that came out of local workshops to be sold to tourists, dustily on display around the room, were their rice and dal, but the occasional major pieces sold to IndoArt International were their wedding feasts.

He had a problem right now, however. The piece she was interested in was not available. The reason it was not available was that he had either loaned it or sold it, he wasn't sure which, but in either case he had lost control of it. He had withheld this detail from his nephew, hoping to solve the problem before he had to look this important client in the eye. But it hadn't yet worked out.

After a bit of obligatory friendly chitchat, Seema came to the point. "I have a purchase order here for item KK329." She didn't want Rakesh to figure out much about the actual object. "I expected that I would be able to pick it up in Delhi by now, but I understand there is some problem." That she had come all this way to deal with the matter in person was both a good sign and a bad sign.

"Yes." He paused, he waved to his nephew to bring forward three chairs, he gestured to a chair for Seema, and sat down heavily himself. "There was a misunderstanding. You see, this is no simple sculpture. I'm sure you understand better than your Christian boss, because you are a Hindu girl. There are some who say such items should not leave the country."

Seema didn't like Rakesh hearing this. "Yes, yes." She waved at the array of carved deities on the counters along the wall. "The gods and goddesses come and go constantly. Where would we be if they didn't?" She laughed. "We sell our culture, the gods get a trip to England or America!"

"May it do them some good!"

"The gods or the Americans?"

"Both! Everyone benefits!" Everyone laughed.

"Well, but you see," said Lal Ram, returning to the point, "this one is not like these. When we received this shipment, it was just before Durga Puja. We thought, why not benefit from this wonderful visitor to our house? And so, we cut our goat in her presence."

"And your family has had blessings ever since. I have heard about this already," said Seema. Lal Ram glanced at his nephew.

"And then, after Durga Puja was over, I was visiting with my Gurudev in his place here, to get some advice about some matter." He waved off that matter as of no relevance to the story. "Gurudev was interested in Kaliji."

Seema winced and glanced at Rakesh, who was listening with great interest.

"He wanted to pay a visit. Can one say no to one's Gurudev? Not possible. So he came. He thought she was very beautiful. He asked about her, where did she come from, how old was she, why did I have her, was I going to keep her. I gave simple answers to these questions. Then he said he would like to have this Kaliji for his temple. I said another party was interested, it wasn't available. I have other beautiful Kali's, I said, but he insisted he only wanted this Kali. How much does your other party offer? He would meet that, plus more." He shrugged and spread his hands to demonstrate the impossible situation he had found himself in. "What could I do? My Gurudev."

Seema was nodding, getting the point.

"What did you tell him about this Kali? Did you tell him its history?"

"I said only it came from Kamakhya. This made him even more interested. About its history, I said nothing. Maybe it was made in a workshop there, maybe not so long ago, who knows?"

"Yes, who knows?" said Seema. "But I need to know more about your source. In my business, I have to track the history of these things."

"I will tell you my source, that is not a problem. We have an emporium in Gauhati, and people bring in things. All kinds of things. Why, you are going there?"

"Yes. Now, about your gurudev."

"I am having very bad feelings, deceiving my gurudev." He laid his hand on his heart to indicate his guilt and grief.

"So then, you let him have it?"

"I said, 'only because you are my Gurudev, I can make a loan. But it is only for a short time. I cannot promise it longer than one year.'"

"One year!"

"Or maybe less time," he hurried on, "if I can find a replacement. So that is what I am now trying to do. I have commissioned a sculptor here in Banaras to make a copy of it."

"Ah! Not a bad idea. How will he do that? Do you have photos?"

"Yes, of course. I have a set of photos – very professional! – from every angle. I made them to give to the sculptor, and also made another set for you." He lifted himself from his chair and rummaged around behind the dusty counter until he found a manila envelope. "For you," he said, handing the envelope to Seema.

She opened it, drew out the envelope, looked through six color photos, drew her breath. "Divine! Absolutely divine." Rakesh leaned in to have a look. Seema resisted the urge to pull them away from him. It was too late now. "How long til the copy is done?"

"Not long. It's getting close to done now. I check every few days, just to keep the man going. No holidays."

"When it's done, how are you going to make the trade?"

"I will tell him we have a better one. No flaws. Even the heel will be perfect."

Seema examined the photos again, carefully, inch by inch. "It looks almost perfect." In one photo, a close-up of Kali's forehead, there seemed to be a nick or a dimple, perhaps where a stone might have chipped out a bit of marble. She peered closely, frowned. "What is this?" she asked, pointing at the spot.

"That is a hole."

"How deep is it?"

"Very tiny hole. It goes all the way through."

"What?!" Seema looked up at Lal Ram.

"Yes," he grinned. "All the way through. To the back of her head."

Rakesh began to laugh. Then Seema joined him, and then, seeing how it was going, Lal Ram and Mohan Ram joined in.

"You've got to be kidding!"

✲ ✲ ✲

Seema flew back to Delhi the next day, while Rakesh, with no expense account, returned to the same city by train. He had tried to get more information about the image from Seema, but all he could get her to say was that it was a good piece, not too old, not really that precious, but buyers in the West were interested in such pieces if it was in good condition, and of course it was all totally legal. He didn't believe her. He knew about the illicit trade in antiquities, and he was certain that her boss was involved in it. He would never, ever report it, but he was fascinated by how the system worked and how much money was involved. He suspected it was a lot. There were billionaire Indian businessmen popping up all over the world, with no imaginable way to spend their billions and wanting to keep their cultural ties to India alive. He knew this, and in fact he wouldn't mind being one of them.

He was part of a small group of musicians who hung out at a place called Netizen, a bar that had evolved from an internet cafe that had evolved from a sleazy 1980s nightclub. He wasn't exactly one of the musicians, but he was friends with some of them, and this place was close to the university. You could go there to study in the early evening, and later on the music picked up. It wasn't a dance hall, mostly, and not many girls hung out there. Hindutva thugs liked to wander in, check out the scene with arms-crossed disapproval, and wander back out. There had been a couple of girls on Valentine's Day who stopped by with their boyfriends for an hour. The thugs were on heightened alert that day, searching out lovers and "bad girls" who were out in public with boys they weren't married to. They found these two girls and attempted to drag them out into the street, to make an example of them. That had provoked a mini riot in the bar, as the locals tried to protect the girls. It was in the papers the next day, along with similar episodes happening all around Delhi. After that, it really became a no-go zone for Delhi's college girls.

But Rakesh still liked it. You could meet the occasional foreigner, guys from the UK or Australia or the US checking out the music scene. They'd hang around for a few weeks, then disappear.

One night, not long after his return from Banaras, he was having a beer with a friend when a couple of Angrezi sauntered in. Before long, they were talking. Mostly IT stuff. The guys seemed to be computer engineers up from Bangalore. They wondered if they should take time for a side trip to Banaras. Rakesh said yeah, if you're into religion, no better place to see Hinduism in action than in Banaras, also known as Varanasi, also known as Kashi. He could hear himself go into Hindu Native mode, and he tried to check himself before he was telling myths and talking about yoga. Instead, he decided to diss the Hindu side. He began talking about fake yogis, fake gurus, fake idols. The two Angrezi were getting into it, laughing and asking for more.

"People really eat this up," said the Brit.

"Are you kidding? Fake idols? How can an idol be fake?" said the Yank.

Rakesh found himself telling about the Kali image that 'someone he knew' was selling to an underground arts dealer who traded in antiquities. He avoided mentioning any names, but the image was old, he knew that. It came from a place called Kamakhya, one of the most famous Tantric places in India, off in Assam in the east. The Brit and the Yank didn't have to ask what Tantra was.

"What's fake about it?" the Yank persisted.

"It has a tube in it. Goes from back of the head to the forehead. You can make it bleed or sweat or spout sacred ash!"

"No way!"

"I'm telling you the truth, man. Believe it or not."

CHAPTER 11

A LATTE

The next morning Annie sipped a cup of milky tea in the quiet refuge of her small room, when the air was still cool and fragrant, and the only sound was noisy blackbirds behind the ashram arguing over scraps of food.

The excitement in the meditation hall had gone on much longer the previous night, and she had stayed until the hall was largely emptied out, not wanting to miss anything that might happen, and in particular to see what the Swami would do. He left shortly after the discovery of the blood on Kali's face and after pranaming to her. Little Tyagi Ma was left looking bewildered among the images she had been serving, gazing out into the crowd of fervent worshippers. Narayan, too, continued to sit at his post beside Swamiji's seat. Annie watched him closely; no telling what he was thinking.

Just as she was leaving the hall, Narayan appeared beside her, startling her.

"Don't be afraid, Annie," he said, which annoyed her.

"I'm not afraid. I'm amazed."

"Tonight we have seen the power of our Goddess."

"It certainly seems so," she said noncommitally.

Narayan's shiny face was close to hers. "You, I think, have some powers as well."

Annie could only tilt her head in puzzlement.

"Isn't it?" he pushed.

"Why do you say so?" she asked.

He smiled enigmatically. "People come here for different reasons. Some come for darshan of Swamiji or Deviji. But also, power draws power. It concentrates in certain places." He waggled his head from side to side in that characteristic Indian way as if he were enunciating a widely known principle.

"Is that so?"

"I am thinking you know this already."

"Really, I didn't."

"You have come here for some reason. Everyone does. But what is your reason?"

"I'm not one hundred percent clear about that."

He smiled and pounced. "You see! This is often the way it is. People come, they don't know why."

Annie was finding him alternately smarmy and sinister. She tried to figure out what he was driving at. She was still pondering that next morning over her tea. The mage talk may be producing some kind of aura about her that would be hard to live up to—or live down, for that matter.

Or did Narayan know about the stone in her possession? It was still in her suitcase, in its red cloth, inside a white pillowcase. It would not be difficult for them to have searched her few things and spotted it. Or was it even still there?

Annie pulled the suitcase from under her bed and opened it. Yes, the white bundle was still there. She felt for the irregular shape of the stone. She felt some relief, but also renewed anxiety about it. She had not yet learned why Shobha had needed to send it out of the country for safekeeping; she had not learned where Shobha was right now. Was she in Kamakhya, as the four sisters thought? But they had also seen her on the back road. She was still afraid to mention Shobha's name or even to ask the sisters more about the missing renunciant even though they themselves had brought her name up. On the other hand, she had no reason to think anyone was looking for the stone.

Still, she felt an urgent desire to hide it better.

✵ ✵ ✵

Little Tyagi Ma appeared in Annie's doorway, looking even more disheveled than she usually did in the morning before having her shower and re-braiding her long gray hair. Her sari was tied tight around her tiny waist, and she was carrying her morning tea.

"Good morning, Mataji," Annie said.

"Oh, oh, yes, good morning Annie. Are you well?" Tyagi Ma always seemed slightly flustered.

"Yes, well enough."

"After last night! It must be so difficult for you, not knowing our religion well." Tyagi Ma seemed distraught about her religion's recent events.

"I have to admit I am a little puzzled."

"Not just you, Annie, not just you!"

"What do you mean?"

Tyagi Ma shook her head in bewilderment. "All these *shakt* things! We never used to have this."

"No?"

"No! We were always Vaishnavite. We worshipped Lord Krishna. We were bhaktis. Lord Krishnu and our guru, that was who we worshipped. It was gentle and joyful. Now all these changes have come!"

"How long has this been going on?"

"The last year, only! Swamiji has brought these changes to our ashram. Why, I can't say. He is so much wiser, I cannot question his doings, because he is my guru, you know, only I just don't understand. He doesn't explain to us. But these strange things are happening!"

"You don't believe in Kali?"

Tyagi Ma looked startled. "Of COURSE I believe in Kaliji! She is the MOST POWERFUL Goddess!" She paused as if to be sure Kali herself heard her saying this. Then she continued, "Only thing is, Kali was not here so much in the past. Krishna was here, and Radha. This place was built by people who wanted to worship Lord Krishna, not by people who wanted to worship Devi. There are other places for that. There are other places where Kali has always been, from ancient times, where her power has always been manifest."

They sipped their tea in silence, pondering the alarming recent developments. Annie was sitting in her armchair, Tyagi Ma on the bed. The suitcase with its white parcel was still standing open on the floor at Tyagi Ma's feet.

"Brahmananda Ma says Kali has come on Her own. That is why this is so disturbing. Kaliji has come, she wants to be worshipped here. She wants this ashram for herself."

"Do goddesses do that?"

"Who knows the ways of the Goddess?"

"Does Krishna just let this happen?"

Tyagi Ma looked at her. "I don't know. The *murti* of Kali in the meditation hall is new. It just came a few months ago. There was a ceremony, Tantric priests came to welcome her. Before, it was Krishna there. And now, this blood! It proves she has come."

"Does it? You were up close. Could you see anything?"

Tyagi Ma appeared to wince. "The lights went out. I saw nothing. When they came back on, the blood was there, that's all I know."

"You didn't see anything else?" Like someone splashing chicken blood on the face of the image, Annie was thinking.

"Yes, there was a bright light moving around the room. Very bright! First it touched the face of Kali, and then Swamiji."

"Hmmm."

"You must have seen it!"

"Yes, now that you mention it, I did see it."

"Things like this never used to happen."

When Tyagi Ma left to take her bath, Annie returned to the problem of a better hiding place for the stone in the pillowcase. If even Shobha had not been able to imagine a safe place in the ashram for it, Annie would not be able to. Where else, then? Dig a hole in the forest? She'd probably never find it again. She had heard about caves upriver on the eastern bank; she could imagine hiding it in one of those. Then of course some spelunking tourist would come along and find it. Or else some sanyasi would take up residence and claim to have discovered the goddess in his cave. Was there anyplace down in town? In one of the hotels, for instance? No, she couldn't trust the hotel staff.

It was Karen's Danish friend who had sent the message on behalf of Shobha, and Annie had not yet made an effort to find her. She remembered that she had an actual address for her. It was time to find Erika Jakobsen.

There is a little enclave of long-term European residents on a small hill above the western bank of the river, where cheap rooms can be rented by the week and leafy open air cafes offer thick black coffee – real coffee, not Nescafe – and crusty bread, cakes, and other comfort foods that Western palates begin to long for after months of chapattis and curry and tea. After not finding the address she was looking for, Annie decided to treat herself to a latte in one of the little cafes. There were cute little red-painted bistro tables and unsteady folding chairs that wobbled on the cobblestone patio.

"What can I get ya?" the perky waitress asked in a distinctly American accent. She was wearing a crumpled salwar-kameez in a faded print.

"I'd love a latte," said Annie.

"Hey. American."

"Yep."

"Where ya from?"

"Seattle, more or less. Where are you from?"

"Portland! We're neighbors. I'm Lonnie."

Lonnie returned with the latte, then sat down on the other wobbly chair. "There aren't that many Americans here," she said.

"Why not?"

"No idea. It's all Europe and Australia. Funny."

"I'm looking for a Dane. Do you know Erika Jakobsen?"

"Sure. She hangs out around here. Usually. Right now she's gone on pilgrimage up to Badrinath. Why are you looking for her?"

"Damn. A friend of mine told me to look her up."

"Well, it'll be several weeks till she gets back. Are you an art historian too?"

"Uh, no. I'm just. . . on vacation."

"Where are you staying?"

"Bhav Dham Ashram."

"Oh! You're THERE?"

"Yeah. Why?"

"Weird things going on there, right?"

"I guess so. Pretty unusual, at least compared to what I'm used to. What have you heard?"

"I've heard their swami is into girls."

"What??"

"Pretty young nuns, getting spiritual powers from The Man." There was a distinct sneer in her voice. "Haven't you seen anything?"

"Not like that. I'm the wrong demographic, myself."

"Don't be too sure!" she laughed.

"Tell me what you've heard."

"Well, I've heard that he picks good looking girls who come for the spiritual life and he gives them a whole lot more than they are looking for. He's doing some Tantric thing with them, you know, waking the kundalini serpent and opening the cakras, and the mind-blowing climax that's a whole lot like orgasm, except it isn't? It's kinky religion. A lot of people are interested in this." She glanced around the empty courtyard.

"How do you know this?"

"There was this girl from the ashram who was hiding out up here. She was getting involved in it, he was putting pressure on her, and she didn't like it. It didn't make her feel spiritual, it made her feel dirty. She still felt it was real, somehow, but she didn't want to be part of it, and she was afraid of the swami."

"Do you know him? Have you seen him?"

"Yeah, the eyes?! I know him. Scares the shit out of me, pardon the language."

"What was this girl's name?"

"Umm, see if I can remember. She went away after a while. Not sure where."

"Was it Shobha?"

"Yes! Shobha. Beautiful girl with wonderful eyes. Just the type a lecherous swami would want in his midnight rituals. She's a friend of Erika's."

"Would she have gone on pilgrimage with Erika?"

"I don't know. Maybe."

Back in her room, Annie checked to be sure the suitcase was still under her bed. Then she opened it to peak in. The lump in the pillowcase was still there. She thought about asking Lonnie to safeguard it for her, and then she thought that Shobha could have asked her, too, but didn't, so why would she do what Shobha didn't think was a good idea?

Annie sighed. There didn't seem to be anything further to do other than continue to follow the one-tongue principle. That meant back to all the daily routines, including the evening satsang, and hope something would break. She glanced at her computer textbooks in the little niche beside the bed. It didn't seem like she was going to be making much progress there, either.

CHAPTER 12

KAMAKHYA

The hired BMW wound up a dry hillside high above the Brahmaputra River, along the stretch where it flows east to west before it turns southward toward Bangladesh and the Bay of Bengal. The vehicle's destination was a site with some similarity to Rishikesh, albeit on the opposite side of India and on a different river, also flowing out of the Himalayas. Along the hairpin turns, red-robed sadhus with red forehead markings and dreadlocks piled like turbans above leathered faces plodded uphill, pulled toward the center of Tantric worship. From inside their air conditioned car, Nic and Seema observed these holy men with something between fascination and dread.

Seema had prevailed on Nic to join her on this trip. "This isn't the kind of place a woman wants to go to alone," she had said. "You don't understand these tantrics. It's all sadhus living in their sexual imaginations, right there at the yoni of Mahashakti." She shivered at the thought of the inner life of these shakt holy men.

All this sounded interesting to Nic, who had been many places in India but never to Assam, even though some of his ancestors had invested in tea plantations there. As they passed through a yellow plastered archway and into the car park of the famous Kamakhya Temple, they saw the beginning of the usual crowds, even though the big festival celebrating Devi's menstruation was still weeks away. The driver swerved to avoid a goat, which was balking at walking across the hot pavement to the place where it was going to be beheaded as an offering to Devi.

"This is going to be fun," Nic said, while unbending himself from the car onto the steaming tarmac. He was dressed in a now-rumpled white kurta with a thin cotton shawl, the standard dress of Western devotees. Seema assumed sarcasm, but thought overall the experience would be good for him.

Passing by a carnival of ritual paraphernalia shops, tea stalls, exotic ascetics, and whole families of devout worshippers and their mostly docile sacrificial victims, they joined the short, five hundred rupee line, rather than the enormous free line, to begin the journey from the upper temple compound into the dark cave of Devi's hidden place. Along the fringes of these queues more red-robed sadhus were camped out, an impressive display of bodily mortification and indulgence. Tridents, belonging to Shiva, were the preferred ornaments, pitched into the sand or wound around necks on wires or piercing tongues, marking these men as consorts to Shakti. Like Shiva, they indulged in ganja and alcohol, covered their bodies with ash, wound themselves with chains of rudraksha beads, pierced themselves with little spears, turned their eyelids inside out, stood on one foot or on their heads, zoned out in deepest meditation. It was hard not to stare at them, because these were hardcore Hindu stereotypes, there was everything but beds of nails, even snake charmers were part of the scene.

After passing through above-ground chambers lined with deities and echoing the cacophony of a dozen Indian languages, the queue turned downward, spiraling into blackness, an endless but orderly thrust of bodies down further and further toward the damp central opening of the cave beneath the temple. Nic, who at home had been reading The Hobbit to Isabella and William, thought of finding Gollum searching for his preciousss in the black muck at the bottom. He was carried along by the pressure of the queue, tightly packed one to another, full body to full body, no male and female sides in this sacred crush. He was a head taller than anyone else in the line, so as his eyes adjusted to the glow of a couple of ghi lamps he was looking along the tops of shining black heads, beginning first with Seema's, whose fragrant shampoo sweetened the other smells of body odor and cave musk.

The crowd, as a self-moving block, came finally to the lowest point, and there were murmurs, gasps, cries, and jostling to reach the spot, where priests chanted and protected and controlled access. There was a still dark pool, with a luminescent film and flowers floating on its surface. From a cleft, a trickle of water flowed into the pool, and above it a small shrouded statue, so covered with red and tinselled cloth that its form could barely be seen. Nic fastened his eyes on this, trying to make out what it was, who it was, how excellent its carved form, of what material it was constructed. Nothing could be seen, except that it was small, a foot high at most. He gripped Seema, who said, "Yes, I see." Impossible to say more.

He was shoved into kneeling posture by a priest, and feared falling in, face first. He caught his balance, and did as others did, putting his palm into the water, feeling underneath, reaching toward the form, where beneath the surface a nub of stone could be felt. He looked at the cleft in the rock, the moist, wet yoni of the goddess. He choked, surprised at the sudden emotion he felt at the Source of creation, in Shakti's most intimate spot. Others were having similar experiences, crying or sighing, each person, despite the crowds, alone at the mysterious and intimate center of life deep in the black core of the cave.

The moment went by too fast. The priest sitting beside the pool was receiving gifts of money; Nic laid a fifty rupee note on his tray and received a plop of wet red sindur on his forehead. Then, before he really wanted to go, he was swept up, outward from the cavern, up another winding set of steps, round and round and back out the top.

When they finally reached sun and air, separating themselves from the crowd, they looked at each other, as if startled at the sudden normality. All they could do was laugh.

☆   ☆   ☆

"There was an image there," Nic said.

"I was surprised; I didn't know. I thought it would only be the pool." The day was heating up, and the crowds growing larger. They had stopped to watch the slaughter of goats, whose heads were efficiently severed, one after another, against a marble wall by priests with broad swords, their blood gushing against the wall and into a trough at the base. Seema turned away from the scene. "This is illegal most places."

"So we are to believe that Muslim conquerors tried to put a stop to this," he said, thinking about how HIS Kali had come to be available to him via a trader in Banaras. "I can imagine they were horrified by scenes like this."

Seema bristled with sudden defensive indignation, then let it go. "I guess it would be shocking," she admitted. "But they have holy places too, and holy caves where God's presence can be felt."

"Mohammad received the Koran in a cave."

"Yes! Let's remember that. But they were smashing idols, so the priests must have felt they had to carry off the beautiful Kali until it was safe to put it back, or replace it." Seema was thinking about the protective priests by the pool, whose families had controlled the site for generations. Easy to imagine them bundling up that statue, slipping up the winding stairway, and stowing it in a rice barrel or warehouse until all danger was past. But after a century or two, and five or six generations, maybe the possessors of the image forgot where it had been.

"It would be interesting to talk to these priests," Seema mused. "Their families have run this temple for generations."

"They aren't just temple employees?"

"Some could be, but control of important temples like these run in families with long histories here. These are big, powerful Brahmin families."

"What would be the point? What could you find out?" Nic was interested, but dubious.

"I doubt our KK has really been forgotten." They were standing in the sun beside the BMW waiting for the driver to show up from wherever he had disappeared to.

"Where's the damn driver?" Nic said, using his shawl to wipe sweat off his forehead. There was no shade in the car park.

"He's drinking tea someplace," Seema said, looking around.

"Why do you think it hasn't been forgotten?"

"I think there would be family stories. A legend of a great Kali they once had, or a split in the family long back. Someone stole it or sold it. That 1825 letter that describes it; why is Gray going to send it, then doesn't?"

"What's your theory?"

"Well I don't really have a theory, but it could be the point where there was a family quarrel or crisis over it. Maybe they needed money badly, but couldn't bring themselves to sell it. Someone prevails on someone else to hold off."

"Why didn't they just put it back in the cave?"

"Good question. But it never went back, did it?" Seema was thinking and talking, while pacing around the car, trying to figure out where the driver could have gone for tea. "If you've got a great work of art that an Englishman is willing to pay a lot of money for, you could justify not putting it back in the cave. For that you can use ANY image. Even just a triangular stone is enough. It's still shakti!"

"Hmmm. Interesting point."

"And maybe there was quite a debate about that. A quiet debate, no doubt." Seema's historian's imagination was running off into the past, wanting to uncover the secrets of a large and powerful family, reconstruct the personalities, trace a quarrel that might have gone on for years. A Bengali Brahmin herself, she knew this culture, the way that large families, lineages actually, branch off, nurture their grudges, rise and fall in wealth, boycott and sabotage each other. There was probably a great story there!

But Nic said, "We don't want to go there."

"Why not?"

"Even if you're right, that was then. It was easy to buy these things then. If there are still people who remember it, we don't want them to start thinking about it now."

From across the car park, the driver was heading their way.

"We don't want them to claim it for the temple, do we? That would make a lovely scandal: 'Kamakhya Temple Demands Return of Ancient Murti.'"

"Umm."

"Or here's another one: 'Antiquities Act Breached.'" The Antiquities and Ancient Art Act of 1972 had attempted to halt the flow of Indian works older than one hundred years out of the country. But because those were 'License Raj' days, it set up an elaborate – and corrupt – system of licensing requirements that brought almost all serious collecting to a halt. Even museums and academics despaired of working with these materials. Only businesses like Nic's thrived, as underground as the Kamakhya yoni.

The driver was all apologies as he unlocked the car, but it was far too hot inside to enter. Instead, he opened all four doors and started the engine. Nic and Seema finished their conversation behind the car:

"In fact, we have to have another story in place. You can work it up. It can't have been in the country since 1972, when the act was established."

Seema pouted. "I really wanted to track down that story."

"Well we don't want to get the Brahmins upset, do we?"

"Maybe," she said, already going with the new story, "your ancestor DID get it out of the country. Maybe it's been somewhere in Europe all along!"

Nic laughed. "That's not bad. Let's go with that."

CHAPTER 13

_____ JASWANTI _____

"I am no renouncer. I am a simple hard-working doctor," insisted Dr. Jayanti Gupta in the roof-top waiting room of her Rishikesh clinic. That she was hard-working was obvious; dozens of women and children were sitting patiently on every surface of the small waiting room for their turn to see her. She was wearing a white physician's coat over a white salwar-kameez, her hair pulled back in a bun with streaks of white.

Gitanjali whispered to Annie, "But she HAS renounced!"

"Never mind, then," said Annie to Dr. Gupta. "We are worried about one of the young women at our ashram."

"Well where IS the young woman?" she demanded in her strong voice. "Why don't you bring her here?"

"That's the problem. We can't bring her."

"Why not?" She was all business.

"She is in some kind of state. She just lies on her bed, as if she were only partly conscious. She weeps. She won't eat or talk. Her *guru-behen* are extremely worried about her." Annie gestured at Gitanjali, who stood meekly beside her.

Dr. Gupta squinted. "What ashram are you from?"

"Bhav Dham Ashram."

"Ah!" she exploded. "Uh-huh. Something going on there." She nodded vigorously to herself.

Gitanjali said timidly, "Would you come and see her?"

"Well, as you can see, I am very busy here. These people have many needs and they have been waiting a long time; I can't drop everything and come. But maybe tonight when I finish I can come by."

"That would be wonderful, thank you Dr. Gupta!" Gitanjali said.

✫ ✫ ✫

Jaswanti was still lying on the enormous bed in the room shared by the four young women. All four of them sat on it by day and slept in it by night. Aside from the bed, there was not space for much else in the room. In one corner was an image of Krishna on a small platform with all the signs of loving adoration day and night. Fresh marigolds lay in front of him, and three sticks of incense were still smoldering when Annie and Gitanjali returned from their visit to Dr. Gupta.

Kunjlata was sitting on the floor facing Lord Krishna and doing *jap*, chanting a mantra while counting off the 108 beads of her mala. Sharada was reading softly from the Gita to Jaswanti, who gave no sign of listening. She was lying flat on her back with her head turned toward the single small window in the room, clutching her mala in her right hand. Her eyes were half-shut, her cheeks were wet.

Annie and Gitanjali took in the scene and saw that it had not changed in the last hour. Annie had been drawn into the situation when Gitanjali showed up at her room as she was returning from her unsuccessful search for Erika Jakobsen. "Please come," Gitanjali had pleaded, after describing the state Jaswanti had been in ever since the previous night.

"Has she been like this before?" Annie asked.

"No."

"Never."

Gitanjali and Sharada glanced at each other. "Well, sometimes when she meditates for a very long time, it seems she reaches a level that we don't."

"Yes," whispered Sharada. "She's beyond us in her spiritual path. She goes into *bhav*. We think so, anyway."

"Bhav? What is bhav?"

"How can we explain?" Gitanjali gave it a try. "The great saints reach this state where their concentration is totally on God and all the outside world disappears and they are not diverted in any way. They are conscious only of God. It is total bliss."

"And Jaswanti becomes like this?"

"It seems to us so, Annie. Remember how she was last night? I mean before all those things happened? Just sitting like this. . . " Gitanjali imitated the yogic posture of Jaswanti, the swaying and the moaning, "she was beyond how we were. And she was calling 'Ma, Ma.'"

"Yes, and then she fell backward," added Kunjlata, who had given up her *jap* with all the conversation going on.

Having stayed until the meditation hall was nearly empty, Annie had watched as the three girls tried to get Jaswanti to stand up. She leaned unsteadily on her feet and was about to sink down again, when Narayan appeared just in time to catch her. He had murmured something into her ear, then said to the other girls, "I am just taking her to Swamiji for a blessing." He led her slowly toward the dais, and she followed obediently in her bhav state, leaning on Narayan for support. He turned back to the other three: "You can go. I'll see that she gets back to her room." Jaswanti disappeared with Narayan into a room behind the images of the gods.

Annie had observed the uncertainty on their faces as they watched Jaswanti being led away, but there was no way they could disobey Narayan. Shortly after that, Annie left for her own room.

Back in their room, Gitanjali, Kunjlata, and Sharada had been unable to sleep with all that had occurred during the evening. The sudden dousing of the lights, the strange dancing light that had shone on Kali and on Swamiji, then the main lights back on and the blood on Kali's face, and then Jaswanti's state, and Jaswanti being led away to Swamiji. . . nothing like this had ever happened before. Who could sleep after that? And where was Jaswanti?

Toward morning, Jaswanti had shown up at the door, led by one of the orange-robed women who seemed more a servant of the ashram than a true spiritual aspirant. This woman turned Jaswanti over to her sisters and disappeared without a word. Jaswanti fell on her sisters, hugged them, and sobbed. When they asked her where she had been, she only shook her head and cried more. They laid her down and calmed her, and she had continued in this same state the rest of the day.

✫   ✫   ✫

In the early evening Dr. Gupta arrived, not wearing her physician's coat and her head closely covered by her dupatta.

"I am not welcome here," she muttered to Annie as the door closed behind her. "Let's see this girl."

Dr. Gupta's strong voice reassured everyone. She sat down on the bed beside Jaswanti, whose large eyes were now open and watching the doctor. Dr. Gupta cradled her hand and felt for her pulse. "Um-hmm," she said. She felt her forehead. She put her fingers in the little indentations below her ears. She pulled back each eyelid and had Jaswanti follow her finger as she wagged it in front of her nose. She took Jaswanti's limp hand back into her own competent one and said, "Now tell me what happened last night."

Jaswanti's eyes went to Gitanjali's. "I'll tell you the first part," Gitanjali said. When she got to the part of the story where Narayan led Jaswanti away, Dr. Gupta's eyes hardened. She turned to Jaswanti and said softly,

"What happened in that room, little one? You can tell us about it. We are all friends here."

Tears began pouring from her eyes again. "Swamiji was there."

"What was he doing?"

"He was meditating. In front of Deviji."

"Tell me about Deviji. A murti?"

"Yes, an image. Smaller than the other one."

"I see. Go on."

"They made me sit down beside Devi."

"In front of Swamiji?"

"Yes."

"Anyone else there?"

"Yes."

"Who?"

"Two other men."

"Who were they?"

"I don't know."

"What happened next?"

"They gave me something to drink."

"Um-hmm," nodded Dr. Gupta, as if she had expected this. "Then what happened?"

"They took my clothes off."

The sisters gasped. There was a fresh wash of tears.

"Then they took off their clothes."

The scene before their eyes was so unspeakable that Dr. Gupta's strong voice came as a rush of common sense: "So everyone was sitting there naked?!"

Jaswanti sobbed. Dr. Gupta turned to look at Annie as if to say, "Can you believe this?!"

"And they did puja next, is that right?"

"Yes. They put flowers in my hair. They worshipped me."

"You understand why they did this, don't you?"

Jaswanti nodded. "They said I was Deviji."

"That's right. And you know, little one, that it is true. All women are Devi in some way. But what they did was not good. Devi does not ask for this. You are not to blame. Do you understand?"

Jaswanti nodded.

"Now I must ask you another question and you must answer. Did anything else happen? Did they do anything else to you?"

Jaswanti shook her head. "No," she whispered. "I just stayed like that for a long time. I began to dream."

"Yes, child. That was the drug. They gave you bhang to drink. You must never take anything they give you." Dr. Gupta looked up at the others. "They drugged her."

She sat there for a long time, watching Jaswanti, patting her hand, soothing her. Finally she turned to Annie, and said: "This is how our Hindu religion can be abused. These young girls come here fleeing marriages they don't want from places where there is no alternative life for a girl. They just want to be good Hindu girls, worship Lord Krishna, live simply in this community, guided by a guru whom they can trust. And they encounter these. . . these scoundrels!"

Gitanjali and Kunjlata gasped. Dr. Gupta raised her hand: "I know, I know. Those are shocking words. But I don't regret them."

Before she left, she took Annie aside for a private conversation.

"How do you come to be here, Annie?"

"I've come on an errand for a friend of mine, an anthropologist."

"Are you here seeking enlightenment?"

"Well, not really, or . . . perhaps only in a general way. I'm not a serious renunciant, if that's what you mean."

"Perhaps I put it badly. So many westerners come here and get caught up in it all. They are enthralled by what this swami is doing, when he is doing a great deal of harm." She nodded toward Jaswanti. "The reason I ask is that we have to protect this girl. Last night was just the start. She wasn't raped, but next time, who knows? This is nothing but temple prostitution. These rituals go a lot further before they are done. This has to be stopped. I'm not welcome here, either. Could you spend the night here? Raise a ruckus if they come for her?"

"Certainly." The bed wasn't really big enough for five, but Annie could sleep sitting up, she thought.

"Girls," Dr. Gupta said to the four of them, "Annie is going to spend the night here. She's watching out for you. Don't leave this room. Don't go anywhere. You understand?"

They all nodded soberly. Gitanjali said, "Good, we'll have our mage with us!"

"We should talk again soon," Dr. Gupta said before she left.

CHAPTER 14

A LONG NIGHT

S o Annie sat up all night in an armchair, looking over four young women the age of her own daughter. Funny how these Indian girls were always called "girl"—*larki*—if they were unmarried, never mind how old they were. Of course, these girls were supposed to be married by now, in their early twenties. But it wasn't going to happen, so how long would they go on being called "girl"? Eventually they would be as old as Tyagi Ma; at some point they would transition to "mother," without the intervening variable of childbirth.

Of course, Annie couldn't help thinking of Jen as still a girl, also. In the long hours of the night she missed that girl, her daughter. So far she hadn't gotten to Rishikesh town to find an internet connection so she could email that she was okay. She had tossed her iPhone into the bottom of her suitcase, next to the stone that was the cause of all this disturbance in her life, in order to prevent herself from accruing data charges, which she knew would be out of sight from India. She had resisted even the quickest, tiniest Facebook post that would let everyone know where she was. Jen might be terribly worried about her, and so would Sam, her son, but she wasn't going to think about that. Jen and Sam were the pull of the old life, and this was the new one. If she started thinking about them, she would start to miss them, then she'd get homesick, then she'd miss her house on the water, and maybe even start to miss Ted. No, she had renounced all that, and she wasn't looking back.

Now she was sounding just like these girls asleep in the big bed. She, too, was a renouncer. Strange. They too had run from family life, from husbands they didn't want. But they had known what they were running to, and Annie didn't. Bhav Dham Ashram was an accident, a temporary stopping point while she figured out the rest of her life, but she surely wasn't getting any 'life work' done here. She was still determined not to let the programming idea go cold, but so far there had been no time for getting out the books. This desire to master programming had something to do with liberation, but she couldn't quite work out the underlying logic of it.

Jaswanti shuddered in her sleep and seemed about to wake up, but after a minute she was quiet again. Annie pictured the scene Jaswanti had described earlier, the swami and two men gazing at this innocent young girl, nude and drugged. It was porn under spiritual cover. Annie had no sympathy for it, she could not bring herself to respect the religious ideology that tried to lift it above what she was certain it really was: fancy porn. She supposed she should get out the book on Hindu renunciation she had bought in Delhi and read up on this, but she had a materialist bent that was more than a "streak": it was bedrock in her character.

Who were the other two men? She doubted Narayan was one of them; he served the master, he didn't join him. Swamiji has a large following, it could have been any of these men. There were those rapt faces during the audience on the roof top, the one thousand rupees per lifetime membership. Does that get you a ritual with a nude virgin?

Probably not. Those people on the roof were probably economy class disciples. The two men with the swami and Jaswanti must be in first class. Do they have greater spiritual achievements or do they just pay more money? Maybe both? Annie wanted to know who they were.

There were a whole lot of things she'd like to get to the bottom of, in fact, but it might take time. She was living in Bhav Dham Ashram on borrowed time, she didn't really know how much of it she had. Maybe they were watching her to determine whether to allow her to stay on. Or maybe she needed to make a donation? If she began to appear to be a cynic or a troublemaker, she could be evicted quickly.

Why had they let her in in the first place? She thought back to that morning on the roof at Swamiji's audience. It had been the "vision" he had pulled out of her, the mage story, that had been decisive. Narayan brought it up again two nights ago, the night of Kali's blood. Both Tyagi Ma and these sleeping girls had heard about it, so the news must have swept through the ashram. Her mage credentials were all she had going for herself. Better not to waste them.

By 4:30 in the morning, when the first green parrots began chattering in the treetops, Annie opened her eyes from a position on the floor. Sometime in the long night she must have abandoned the chair for a more comfortable posture, even though the mat was hard. The four young women were already doing *jap* in front of Lord Krishna. Their soft, rapid utterances created a hum, even a vibration, in the room: *Om Namo Bhagavate Vasudevaya,* over and over and over. It was for this they had given up marriage and family life. Elsewhere all over India, young wives were making chapattis, feeding babies, sweeping courtyards, getting the day started; the worker-women of the species hard at work. Here, the cosmos is fed by the mindful concentration of a few who long only to be fully at home in it, conscious only of God.

Jaswanti was no longer weeping, but sleeping peacefully and in no immediate danger, so Annie quietly crept out of their room and made her way back to her own.

She pulled out the book on Hindu asceticism, and leafed through the pages, studying the illustrations. She stopped here and there to read: "Shakti means literally energy, the energy of the universe, of the entire cosmos. Shakti, like electricity, must be controlled by the aspirant, otherwise it is worthless or dangerous."

The book explained that in some sects the aspirant seeks union with the cosmos through a sexual metaphor, in which the ego, the self, is female and the cosmos is male. And in the *panchamakara* ritual, the female is the fire into which the male offers semen, just as clarified butter is offered in ordinary fire worship.

She had read about these "Left-Handed" practices in graduate school, but there had been a theoretical quality to them, something that was practiced in former times and was of great interest to a certain kind of Victorian gentleman. Could anybody be doing this with a straight face today?

✩ ✩ ✩

Annie decided to establish a routine for her life in the ashram, the better to see and to be seen. The one place she could be sure of seeing Swamiji each day was at his morning audience; she began going to all of them. Her presence was generally noted by a nod from Swamiji and a smile from Narayan. She was prepared with more dreams in case he tried to pull another from her, but he didn't.

She also decided to spend more time in the meditation hall in addition to evening satsang. There was always a lot of coming and going here. Travelers stopped by, tourists came in and looked around, various hangers on always seemed to be around and have an angle. Once a young man introduced himself to her and insisted she follow him. First he made her do a full, face-down prostration before the image of Kali; then he took her on a walk to a temple on the wooded hillside above the road into town, where a priest put a dot of sandalwood on her forehead, expecting a few rupees in return; then, as Annie was growing suspicious about where it all was leading, the young man asked her for money. "Sorry, you see I have no purse with me," she said, and walked back to the ashram alone.

To justify time in the meditation hall, she was going to have to do *jap*. She doubted she could do five thousand or a thousand or just one hundred and eight like everyone else, but she was determined to give it a try, and who knew what might come of it?

But what would her mantra be? She understood she needed one; almost everyone at the ashram got theirs from Swamiji. But the thought of going to him, requesting a mantra or to be accepted as his disciple. . . besides not knowing the protocol for this kind of action, she profoundly did not want to submit herself to another man so soon after having left her own domineering husband. That was exactly the sort of thing she had renounced.

She tried out some chantable phrases from her own background. "The Lord is my shepherd." "Hail Mary, full of Grace." It seemed disrespectful to both faiths. She decided just to work through the beads and move her lips.

✩ ✩ ✩

For the next few weeks Annie never missed the rooftop audience. It seemed like a constant cycle of new faces, presentation of fruit, sweets, and envelopes, requests for advice about marriage matches, coming retirements, business plans. Occasionally Swamiji would say, "Let us talk further," and that seemed to mean, later on in private. Narayan was always at his side, managing people, making receipts, often speaking for Swamiji when he lapsed into inscrutable silence. Occasionally Swamiji seemed annoyed, and once or twice positively angry.

There was one five-day period when Swamiji was "indisposed," but spoke through a speaker from his chambers. Narayan would accept the gifts, tell swamiji who the donor was, and relay apologies that the master ill, but "nothing serious." A week later there was another miracle to report: the master had been in two places simultaneously, Rishikesh and Banaras. Since only Annie had sat through all the mornings on the rooftop during both weeks, only she had the perspective needed to wonder: "Surely he was just on the phone from Banaras!" But the story gained momentum, it established credibility, and soon was repeated with fervor and amazing embellishments.

It was after one of these rooftop events that Annie encountered Narayan on her way to the meditation hall.

"You are becoming a devoted follower of the master, Annie."

Annie smiled. "I think he is an amazing person."

"Yes! This is what everyone knows."

"So many new followers. It seems that there are new people every morning."

"Swamiji is becoming very popular. He now has two other ashrams, in Banaras and Kamakhya."

"I have heard he can be in all three places at once. Is this true?" Annie tilted her head with curiosity.

"It is true! Only a VERY great swami can do this." But Annie thought his eyes flickered a little as he spoke.

"Why is this growing so fast?"

"It is the blessing of Deviji. She has selected Swamiji because of his great devotion to her. She is pouring out her love and favors on him and his followers. This is what people are hearing and this is the reason they are coming to see him." Narayan was earnest and fevered in his explanation. "There are not many places where She comes these days, with all the films and television and loudspeakers that distract people from God. She desires to be worshipped again as before. Swamiji is becoming Her favorite connection to people."

Annie walked slowly back to her room, crossing the courtyard and thinking carefully about the unfolding events. This was actually a pretty interesting place to be. Swamiji was an ambitious man, and clever besides. How far could he take this? Were tours of Europe and America ahead?

CHAPTER 15

SEARCHING FOR GURUDEV

S eema decided she was willing to risk exposure of her relationship with Nic for the opportunity of spending some golden days with him back in Banaras. They found a small hotel at Assi Ghat on the river, just upstream from Manikarnika Ghat, where there was little traffic and it was unlikely anyone from her family would spot them. Nic had convinced her that they should end any further snooping among the original custodians of Kamakhya Kali, and focus on finding its current possessor – Lal Ram's gurudev.

Lal Ram had discouraged this very effort by refusing to reveal the name of his gurudev, feeling convinced that a snooping Brit could blow the whole thing up. Nic was pretty sure the whole deal was going to dissolve by attrition if he couldn't figure out a way to goose the process a bit. That was how he ended up in a small but quaint room with Seema, with unreliable AC and service, overlooking the Ganges.

Seema and Nic were in no hurry to get out of their room early for viewing the sun coming up over the river or rowing down to Manikarnika Ghat, as nearly everyone else in the hotel was doing. They were absorbed in more intimate thrills.

Pillow talk had a way of always turning to Kamakhya Kali, their great project. There were no other big life projects available to them. They would never have a home together, never any children, never any shared group of friends, never any network of relatives. Their togetherness consisted of the Nehru letters, the KK project, and the project after that.

Seema was staring at the ceiling while Nic was slowly re-awakening. She had her arms behind her head, her hair sprayed out whichever way, a sheet pulled up modestly over her bare breasts and tucked under her sides. "How about this," she started. "KK was brought to London in 1826 by a merchant who purchased it from an impoverished Brahmin family from Gauhati. It was sold to a private collector whose name is in old records, et cetera, to be invented – we can come up with a name – who some time later sold it to someplace in Europe. . . , where there was civil unrest, or war. . ."

"One of the German states, or someplace in Eastern Europe. . . ." Nic was now looking at the ceiling, too. "Have you got a teleprompter up there?"

". . . where it disappeared until very recently, when it came into our hands. And we aren't at liberty to disclose our source." She looked at Nic. "Does this work?"

"It doesn't bear too much scrutiny. There are lots of people like you who like to track things down." He tried tugging at the sheet covering her breasts, but she clinched her arm muscles to hold it in place.

"Well, the Kamakhya connection is a big selling point, I should think. We want to be sure that's part of the story."

"Right. But we won't want the piece attracting a lot of attention. No press releases, no public auction. We don't want your Brahmins finding out about it and getting upset, do we?"

After driving away from the Kamkhya Temple two days earlier, they had had the driver take them to the small temple in the city where Lal Ram's agents reported they had purchased the piece from the priest. It was a small and ugly temple, more of a shrine than a temple, tucked behind a tree that grew up at the edge of a busy marketplace. The tree was lifting pavement all around, and wires passed through its middle limbs connecting shops and flats to a single telephone pole that was matted with illicit wires. The little mold-streaked temple had an iron gate that protected the current deity, an ugly plaster Durga who appeared to be quite popular locally, judging by the array of gifts – fruit and blossoms, mostly – and the attentiveness of the priest. This was the kind of place Nic would never have stopped to look at; in fact, would not even have noticed, had anything drawn him to this street, which nothing would have.

Seema struck up a conversation with this priest, who was happy to talk about his little shrine. She was good at this; she could get people to talk about anything. Nic let her talk, and anyway he could not follow the conversation, which was in Bengali rather than Hindi. Seema told the priest that she had come to this temple twice before, and there had been a beautiful Kali; that was why she brought this Angrezi. She wanted to show him. Where had it gone? Before long, he was telling her the whole story. Now and then she'd stop and give Nic a brief summary, from which he surmised she was getting to the bottom of things.

"This man is related to the Kamakhya priests," she reported, breaking away from the conversation briefly with a gleam in her eye, then dipped back into the Bengali conversation. Nic stood politely by, as if he understood every word, but he was eyeballing the ornamentation of the room, the ugliness of the image, the calendar art reproductions of Ganesh and Shiva, the splashes of sindur and sandal-wood, the burnt down incense. "The rich side of the family is angry with him," she reported next. "They quarreled." Nic liked the looks of this priest, who seemed both intelligent and dignified. Seema was nodding repeatedly and muttering, "achcha," all full of sympathy about the story she was hearing.

Eventually Seema was finished with the priest's account, and there were pro-longed and grateful farewells, after a dab of sindur onto each of their foreheads. Their car was waiting for them on the street, but Seema wouldn't repeat any of it in the car where the driver might hear. When they finally got to their hotel room, she filled him in triumphantly.

"Just as I guessed! Listen to this: KK was in the hands of this family centuries ago after it was hidden away from Muslim conquerors. They knew they had it; they always knew. They worshipped it in their own household until such a time as it could safely go back into Kamakhya Temple. But eight generations ago there was a huge split in the family."

"He knows that precisely? Eight, not nine or seven?"

"Eight! These people know their genealogies. There was a quarrel over land the maharaja had given to support the temple and the Brahmins. It went on and on. In the courts, out of the courts. Finally the other side of the family won the land somehow, by hook or by crook."

"I thought I heard that phrase."

"Yes, he said it in English. But his side was left with Kamakhya Kali. And the other side has been trying to get it back from them for years. In the early twentieth century, the Maharaja of Cooch Bihar finally declared KK was the prop-erty of our guy's branch. There was also something about the Maharaja's family not being able to go to the Kamakhya Temple, or even look at it on the hill, so maybe that was part of their motivation. Anyway, it was settled. What could they do?"

"So, it was his to keep or to sell?"

Yes. Apparently there had been an earlier attempt to sell it, back in the middle of the big quarrel eight generations ago – and that must be when your ancestor thought he was going to buy it!"

Nic looked at Seema in astonishment. "Brilliant!" He shook his head, amazed. "And why didn't they?"

"There were actual threats against his ancestors by the other side. They insisted that KK go into a public shrine where they could all keep an eye on it."

"That explains this ugly little temple." They both laughed. Seema agreed it wasn't much to look at.

"So why is he selling it now?"

"Well, he has two daughters and no sons. And he wants these daughters to get good educations, university educations. And the only thing he has to raise the money is our KK."

"More brilliant! So it's all going to a worthy cause!" Nic thought a moment. "Wait a minute. Isn't there going to be trouble from the other side when they see that it's no longer where it's supposed to be?"

"That's why they are still angry at him, after all these generations. It was getting too expensive to maintain this shrine, and he always worried about the beautiful Kali being stolen. He informed them that he was 'donating' it to an important ashram. . . in Banaras. And actually, I think he believes that's all he's done. A 'donation' with a nice return gift of cash. But the other side always thought they could get it back. Now it's gone for good."

Nic loved stories like this; it made the antiquities trade a joy as well as a fortune for him. He knew the secret backstories of many important pieces now in the private collections of his patrons all over the world. Sometimes he filled in the new owners, and sometimes he didn't. It all depended on how he read their interests. If he thought they were collecting as investments, he generally didn't tell, because it could make re-sale difficult. When pieces proved to have been acquired illegally, matters could end in complicated lawsuits. But if the collector wanted it because he or she loved it and intended to keep it indefinitely, they might love it better if they knew the whole story. It was tricky to read these clients correctly, but that was part of the fun of the trade.

"Oh, one more thing. The little hole in the forehead?"

"Yeah?"

"He knew all about it, of course, and he claimed he didn't like it one bit. He never used it. But he seemed sure that centuries ago while it was still in place in the big temple, that was when the hole was drilled, so that worshippers could experience the miracle of a little blood on Devi's forehead!"

✿ ✿ ✿

Seema went alone to Lal Ram's warehouse behind Manikarnika Ghat, leaving Nic behind at the hotel. She thought she would have better luck without a foreigner along. She chose a time at mid-afternoon when she thought Lal Ram would be home eating lunch or having a little nap. She discovered, when she reached Lal Ram Import Export Emporium, that she was in luck; no one was there but a young man she hadn't seen before.

"Hello, bhai, is Lal Ramji here?"

"No, memsahib, he is not here." The young man was extremely polite. He introduced himself as Lal Ram's youngest son, Jitan. "But may I be of some service?"

She turned her radiant smile on him. "He is a friend of my family. He has told us about his gurudev, and I told my mother about him, and my mother is very anxious to meet him. There are so many unreliable swamis about, aren't there? But I have such confidence in Lal Ram! I'll just have to come back when he is here. I have come a long way by bus. Unless you could tell me the name of his gurudev?"

"Yes, I can certainly help you with that, memsahib. His gurudev is Swami Shaktinandan in Bhav Dham Kashi Ashram. Do you know this place?"

Jitan got another dazzling smile from Seema. "Oh, achcha, thank you very much, Jitan. You have been very helpful! Yes, I can find it."

✿ ✿ ✿

CHAPTER 16

___ AN IMPORTANT GUEST ___

Once again Annie was heading down to town with her laptop in her shoulder bag, determined to send some emails to Jen and Sam, and find out what had been going on in the outside world. This meant she would be learning about Ted's present state; there was going to be more than one angry flame from him. She had ground her teeth all night against it, accused herself of cowardice and immaturity, and finally resolved to face up to the real world, and the trouble she had stirred up in it.

But at the big iron gate at the back of the ashram, she encountered a commotion of people rushing past her to open it, and she quickly stepped aside, pressing herself to the wall. A large black Ambassador flying small green, white, and ochre flags on both its front fenders drew up and moved quickly in, and just as quickly the gate shut behind it. Instantly men sprang out of the vehicle from all doors; last out was its main occupant, a large man dressed in kurta-pajama with thinning hair that was long enough to curl vainly at his neckline. He smoothed the sides of his hair with his palms as he straightened up. He was perspiring profusely in the mid-afternoon heat and anxious to get into the cool of the ashram, but he returned the namaskars of the people in the courtyard with all the cordiality of someone used to the public eye.

"Who is that person?" Annie asked a young man standing nearby.

"That is Jyoti Prasad, very big politician. He is one of Swamiji's followers."

Narayan, who had come out the door to greet Jyoti Prasad, stood straight-backed with hands clasped in namaskar. Annie never saw him so dignified. In seconds, all the important people had swept inside and the door closed behind them.

☆ ☆ ☆

Dr. Gupta's clinic was crowded as ever with patient women holding listless children, toddlers sucking their thumbs, little girls jiggling restless babies while mothers gazed into space. It was late afternoon, the peak of the heat, and the fan rattled ineffectively on the ceiling. It was a place of desperation and resignation.

"Do you have time to talk today?" read the note Annie sent in to the doctor. Curiosity about the big black car in the courtyard trumped curiosity about Ted.

Dr. Gupta poked her head out her office door and motioned for Annie to come in.

"How is our Jaswanti doing?" she asked, sitting down behind her large desk. In spite of the heat, she appeared cool.

"Seems to be fine. I stop for a visit each day. She seems the most devout of them all."

Dr. Gupta nodded in her confident way. "Yes, there's often a natural inclination in the way these people are made. They go into spiritual states easily. We call this *bhav* in our religion. Many of your Christian saints had this capacity. It may have a physical basis but is given a religious meaning. Above all, epileptics are frequently thought to have great spiritual gifts. One of our greatest recent saints was an epileptic. She also happened to be very beautiful, which may have helped her attract devotees. Now, tell me what's up?"

"Who is Jyoti Prasad?"

Dr. Gupta slapped her pen down. "He is a. . . ," she spluttered for the right word, "a scoundrel of a politician! He's a right wing Hindu nationalist of the worst sort. Why do you ask? Has he come here?"

"Yes, he just arrived at the ashram. He came in a big black car by the back gate and dashed inside."

Dr. Gupta threw herself against the back of her chair and peeled her glasses off, frowning. "Let me tell you about this man." She leaned forward again, elbows on her desk, glasses waving in the air. "Twenty years ago, he was a major player in the Babri Mosque incident. It was in the town of Ayodhya. There was a mosque which was said to have been built by the Mughals over a Hindu temple built on the site of the birthplace of Lord Ram. It all may very well have been true, they did this sort of thing. But Hindus and Muslims lived side by side in that place for centuries, they worshipped side by side, they celebrated many of the same religious holidays. There was peace, let me just put it that way. Peace.

"Then Indian politics found an angle here. The Congress Party had grown corrupt and indifferent, but it stood for low castes and Muslims as well as the interests of the old elite, the Brahmins. It passed liberal reforms on behalf of these minorities, which a lot of people – Hindus – didn't like. So one way to dislodge Congress from power was to appeal to our Hindu identity; this became a movement known as Hindutva, 'Hindu-ness.' And the Babri Mosque became a dramatic symbol for the ambitious politicians of the Hindutva movement. One of the worst of these men was Jyoti Prasad, then a young political operative. He went around the countryside in a caravan, loudspeakers blaring about removing the mosque and re-building the temple of Lord Ram. They raised millions of rupees from rural people to buy bricks to build this temple. And all this effort worked its miracle: in a single day, hundreds of swamis and sadhus and sanyasis converged on the mosque and tore it down. In a single day! Muslims tried to defend it, and there was the usual violence that we have when we all go a little crazy here in this country. Thousands of people died."

"Did the temple get re-built?"

"Not so far! The government has had it sealed off for two decades now." She shook her head at the foolishness of it all. "But in the meantime, these politicians have benefitted enormously, in and out of power, splintering into factions and new parties. This is Indian politics for you, Annie."

"Sometimes I wish we in the U.S. had more than just two parties to pass power back and forth. They are growing more and more alike."

"Well don't look to India for a better model!" They both laughed. "Now, the question is, what is Jyoti Prasad doing with your Swami?"

"'Our swami' is gaining many new adherents, according to Narayan. He's opening new ashrams."

"Is he? Hmmm. I see. This is interesting." She paused to think through what it all might mean. "So Jyoti Prasad has gone *shakt*. Well it makes a certain sense. He wants power, more and more of it. Maybe he's also seeking it by religious means."

"Not that different from politics in my country. Candidates go to prayer meetings, get the support of religious leaders, adopt the agenda of religious conservatives."

"Absolutely! Well, this makes me worry for little Jaswanti again. This man may have come for more than a consultation with the Swami."

"I was just having the same thought," Annie said.

"She really needs to get out of there. It is going to be impossible for her to resist the pressure of her Gurudev. He is all-powerful for her."

Annie suddenly realized what must have happened to Shobha and why she was now on pilgrimage in the Himalayas. She was on the run.

"Even in ashrams, women aren't safe, are they?"

"No. Not even there."

✬ ✬ ✬

Annie went straight to the quarters of the four sisters. Wet saris were draped across the bushes outside their room, drying in the sun. Inside, the room was freshly swept and the little image of Lord Krishna had been washed and worshipped with fruit, and the room was filled with the fragrance of fresh air and incense. Kunjlata was sitting in front of it, beads in hand, rocking back and forth silently, her lips forming the syllables of her mantra. Sharada and Gitanjali were sitting on the big bed, Sharada reading aloud from the Gita.

Annie knocked and entered, took in the scene. "Where is Jaswanti?"

Three sets of eyes turned on her, but no one spoke. Annie waited. Finally, Gitanjali spoke: "They came for her."

"Who came?"

"Brahmananda Ma and Narayan." Brahmananda, one of the widows who lived in the same wing as Annie, always officiously did Swamiji's bidding. She was a large woman with big, sad, puffy eyes, darkly circled, someone who had plainly had a hard life and was now finding respite and satisfaction in her life at the ashram. Annie always felt some sympathy for her, while not exactly liking her.

"We couldn't stop them," Sharada said. "How could we say no?"

"What did Jaswanti say?"

"She said nothing. She obeyed."

"My God."

Kunjlata began to cry.

That evening the meditation hall began to fill up early as news went round that Jyoti Prasad would make an appearance. It seemed everyone knew who he was. The papers were full of his campaign, as his larger-than-life personality made his every move the subject of media chatter. He had been in almost every high level position Indian government had to offer, although at the moment he was without portfolio, which didn't really matter, because his own persona was the biggest portfolio a politician could have. He was campaigning for a seat in the Lok Sabha to replace the one he had lost in the last election, although this was a different seat with a different constituency.

The night was sweltering, since the monsoons were still many days away. The rains had been working their way across North India, beginning three weeks ago in the Sundarbans, moving up to Calcutta two days later, then to Bihar. Every day the papers showed how far they had come across the great Gangetic Plain, and people prayed to Ganga along their own hilly stretch of the river, would she please welcome the rains, and soon. So far there had been no respite from the heat, not even puffy clouds to give hope.

As people settled into positions to begin their meditations, Tyagi Ma could be seen on the dais in front of the deities, arranging offerings, lighting candles and incense, tidying things up. This was her nightly job, a task she loved and protected from encroachment. Kali towered over her, enshrined in the *garbagriha* – the "womb-house" inner sanctum – that cast her in mysterious shadows. The overhead fans were doing their best, as the room rapidly heated, and the loudspeaker system began playing the familiar kirtans, rhythmic music consisting solely of the chanted names of God. Annie, Kunjlata, Gitanjali, and Sharada sat close together near the front of the hall.

Swamiji always sat on a backless Indian-style throne, that now awaited his appearance, while Narayan perched on a small stool placed at his feet. There were several additional seats this evening, no doubt one for Jyoti Prasad and perhaps for other personages from his entourage. Tyagi Ma had disappeared into the shadows among the lesser gods at Kali's feet. Never, from Annie's experience, were there men in rumpled suits, like now, simultaneously invisible and important, standing on the wings of the dais, gazing off into the crowd of worshippers, with lumps under their coats and wires in their ears.

The kirtans and the worshipful chanting grew louder as people sensed the imminent arrival of Swamiji and the celebrity politician, but no one was expecting what came next. Led onto the dais by two saffron-robed sadvis, a small female figure heavily draped in red and gold shuffled forward with difficulty. Impaired by the weight of the robes, she was helped to sit on the central seat directly under Kali. The sadvis arranged her robes and adjusted the gold ornaments in her hair, which flowed loosely across her shoulders and over her chest. Then they namaskared deeply to her, and retreated into the shadows.

"Jaswanti!" whispered Kunjlata, in shock.

"It's Jaswanti!" exclaimed Gitanjali simultaneously.

The meditation hall had gone practically silent except for the continued wheeling of the tape recorded kirtan, as people tried to grasp what was happening.

"Who is she?" people whispered to each other.

With perfect timing – a pause long enough to rivet attention and arouse well-focused puzzlement – Swamiji arrived on the dais, his hands folded in reverent namaskar, his eyes beaming on the small feminine figure. He knelt before Jaswanti, and embraced her feet, an unmistakable act of deep reverence. He was subordinating himself to this figure, who could be none other than an embodiment of divine Kali herself. The sound of the kirtan rose, and the singing began again, though overlaid with the buzzing of astonished whispers as people figured it out, explained it to each other. "Jai Kali Ma!" rose from some voices. Kali had incarnated in this girl!

Finally, the portly figure of Jyoti Prasad appeared. He was wearing a loose shirt over loose pants, both tinted delicately saffron, with several thick garlands around his neck. For once he was not milking the crowd, but appeared fixated on the figure of Jaswanti, avatar of Kali. With folded hands, he walked across the dais to her. He took the garlands from his neck and laid them around Jaswanti's shoulders. Then, with difficulty, he labored down onto his knees to worship her; and next, despite his middle-aged girth and awkwardness, he struggled on down, all the way down in full prostration. Jaswanti at first seemed to gaze into the air over his head, but then looked down at him with an expression of disgust and dread; although it was later said that she had poured out her blessings on him.

Meanwhile, photographers appeared from the sides of the hall, suddenly all over the scene, front, back, and sideways, shooting the prostrate politician, getting up close to the face of the beautiful Jaswanti, shooting over-the-shoulder shots that took in Jaswanti's black hair and Prasad's sparsely tufted scalp, shoe shots that ran up Prasad's legs toward Jaswanti's bowed head. These photographs appeared in all the papers of India the following day, as the Hindu nationalist leader was shown in his prostration before Kali's miraculous incarnation.

At the end of the kirtans, with Swamiji and Jyoti Prasad flanking Jaswanti-Kali, the entire crowd was allowed to pass in front of her to gain her darshan and to touch her feet. No one missed this opportunity, for which Jaswanti had to sit very still, with both sandaled feet exposed to the touch of several hundred people. Her three sisters and Annie were among the first few, before her toes became bruised and sore. As Gitanjali approached her, she tried to perceive what kind of mental and emotional condition Jaswanti was in. She thought Jaswanti looked unfocussed, certainly drugged, and yet the goddess squinted slightly as her eyes met her sister's, as if to send a message. But what that message might be, Gitanjali could not tell.

✳   ✳   ✳

Later that night, in a dark and cooled room, Jaswanti again sat enshrined on a soft mat on which an inverted triangle had been painted. Her feet ached from the patting, pinching, and caressing they had undergone, and her skull felt too small to contain its swollen contents. She was groggy and confused; Brahmananda was ministering to her, removing the heavy veil and sari, now soaked with her perspiration, undoing the choli, loosening the petticoat that held the sari in place. The cool air felt gentle on her skin, and she longed to topple sideways and sleep. The wilted garlands on her chest scented and cooled her bare breasts.

"Stay," hissed Brahmananda before she disappeared through a side door. She reappeared with a brass tray filled with food and drink, which she laid beside Jaswanti's knee, then she left again.

Through another door entered Jyoti Prasad, dressed only in a white dhoti tied around his waist. He sat down, yogi-like, a few inches in front of Jaswanti. Through her befuddled eyes, she saw a rotund belly, a round forehead with hair wet from a bath, round eyes glistening with anticipation. Jaswanti shut her eyes.

"Ah, little Kali Ma," he murmured to her. From the tray he took a brass pitcher of water, and began to sprinkle it on her hair, on her shoulders, on her breasts, down her waist, into the dark space between her folded legs, on her knees and feet.

He took another jug and poured its contents into two cups. One he handed to Jaswanti; but she would not accept it. He took her hand and closed her fingers around the cup, and told her, "Drink." Obediently, she took a sip. "Drink more." He persisted until she had finished it all, then he drank his down in a few gulps.

The effects of the drug, on top of the drug they had given her earlier, made Jaswanti feel she was afloat in some heavenly place. She was said to be a goddess, and she did indeed feel clouds and breezes embracing her. Jyoti Prasad was touching and murmuring things over all the parts of her body, and with her eyes closed and mind floating these sensations were not unpleasant. She swayed, head spinning, and felt she was falling backward, but he caught her, and put his hand in more places where she had never felt human touch. She felt a shock of electricity run through her, the shakti of a goddess awakening in her, and then she swooned again.

A moment came when she felt herself being lifted, moved toward Prasad by someone from behind her who was assisting. Waking again, she could not make out what was happening, she struggled, she cried out, but she was pushed down onto his lap, and she felt herself pierced by something hard and long, "no!" she cried, but there was no way to avoid this embrace, this thing inside her, the powerful arms that encircled her tightly, the unpleasant organic breath on her face, the thick, wet lips that closed over hers, the hairs and belly pressed against her stomach, the sweat that rubbed off on her skin, the fluids that gushed from her vagina.

Prasad enjoyed his ecstatic union with the goddess. Jaswanti was carried weeping from the room to a narrow cot, where she wept the rest of the night.

CHAPTER 17

IN THE NEWS

"Well, well, well!" chuckled Nic. "Look at this." He had finished his English-stye breakfast in the small dining room of the Assi Hotel in Banaras. All the other breakfasters had come and gone, but Nic and Seema were still there, reading the local papers and downing a second pot of tea. Nic folded back the Hindustan Times and handed it to Seema with a rattle of newsprint.

"Jyoti Prasad Worships Devi," said the headline. The photo accompanying the story was not so neutral. Prasad's rear end filled the foreground on the right; it sloped down to his head and prostrate arms in the middle; and on the near right was the beautiful young goddess, Jaswanti Devi. On balance, Prasad cut a comical figure with the prominence of his behind, in contrast to the loveliness of the girl covered in garlands and silk.

"Oh. My. God." Seema laughed aloud, looked up at Nic, then looked down again to read the story. "'Lok Sabha candidate Jyoti Prasad casts aside campaigning for a moment of devotion yesterday in Rishikesh,'" she read aloud. "Oh, sure, this has nothing to do with the campaign. 'The young incarnation of Devi, recently announced by Swami Shaktinandan of Bhav Dham Ashram. . . .' What?!" She looked at Nic again. "Of Bhav Dham Ashram. Swami Shaktinandan. Is that OUR Swami Shaktinandan?"

Nic raised his eyebrows and his shoulders simultaneously. "Look at the photo."

Seema turned back to the photo. On the far left of the photo, raised on a pedestal, were the legs and waist of a black marble deity. Only her practiced eye, closely examining the grainy newsprint image, could have detected the damaged left leg. Nothing above the waist was visible, but this much, combined with the names of the swami and the ashram electrified Seema. "This is KK!" She said this too loud; she glanced around, but the single waiter was standing by the door watching something going on in the hall, then she lowered her voice to say: "This is our man, our swami. He's got our Kali!"

Nic smiled with more restraint: "It appears to be very likely. Now, what do we do about it?"

"We go to Rishikesh."

"This little adventure has turned into quite a holiday. Are we quite done with Banaras?"

"Don't go, then. I'll go by myself." She looked at him tauntingly. "But you'll miss all the fun."

"I wouldn't miss it for the world. I'm having the time of my life." He blew her a kiss, to which she shifted moods.

"I'll see you have a good time."

"Will you! Then it's off to Rishikesh."

Annie was experiencing a surge of revulsion and longing for the normality of her old life on the bay. At home, it could be cool and sunny at the same time. God was wonderfully far away, benign in his heavens, and no one ever claimed to be a goddess – who could even imagine it? This morning she could be having a pleasant pedicure, perfectly harmless and meaningless. She even missed Ted a little bit. She could be planning to grill salmon and maybe Jen and Sam would come for dinner.

Not that she had any intention to go back to that life. But this present one had to be brought to a conclusion so she could get on to the next phase, which required some planning that wasn't getting done. All she really was responsible for in India was getting the red-wrapped stone into Shobha's hands, and then she was finished. She could not rescue Jaswanti; she could not stop Swamiji. People like Jyoti Prasad would continue to do what they had been doing all along, manipulating peoples' emotions by manipulating their most powerful religious symbols, in order to get them to vote for him. His ability to command these supporting troops made him a player in the small world of political competitors, and none of this was ever going to stop.

The day after Jaswanti's presentation and Prasad's prostration, and in the days following, there was intense conversation all over the ashram and in all the other establishments in Rishikesh as the news, followed by additional intriguing rumors of all sorts, went out. There were very few total skeptics like Annie and Dr. Gupta, but many did not like the clout Swamiji was gaining at the perceived expense of other swamis and gurus, or the recognition that was coming to Bhav Dham Ashram. There had been a sequence of manifestations for months that a lot of people outside the ashram knew about, but the incarnation of Kali in beautiful Jaswanti topped everything. Everyone wanted to see her. Even the desperate mothers with the sick children in Dr. Gupta's clinic now had a second line of hope. Where before, everyone who wanted to visit Swamiji during his morning audience had been easily fitted onto the rooftop audience space, now there were lines at the street-side door which had to be controlled.

Swamiji was determined not to let Jaswanti be cheapened by frequent visibility. It was decided that Jaswanti would show herself once a week only, on Tuesdays, and that soon created a sensation as crowds gathered all day for her evening darshan in the meditation hall. The rest of the week, Jaswanti was secluded in a small room with a walled garden guarded with a degree of reverence by the ashram widows. There she attempted to reproduce her daily routine by continuing to lovingly worship Krishna, do 1008 japs a day, take little naps, bathe and wash her sari and change into a fresh one, but without her sister companions, the joy had gone out of her life.

Annie's moment of detachment was not to last. One night after satsang, she came back to her room and found the suitcase lying at an angle under the bed. She noticed this with a shiver of shock, and quickly opened it to see if the stone was missing. But there it was, inside the pillowcase, still in its red shroud, tied with jute string. It may have been altered in some way, as if it had been opened and carefully re-tied, but she couldn't be sure.

She made herself a cup of tea and settled into her lone chair. The door was shut and bolted, and she felt safe. She gazed at the little package, the oddly shaped pillowcase. She had not bothered to look at it the whole time she had been in

India. It had been a mute and muffled presence in her luggage, a responsibility and a weight, an object of value to her only because a girl and a family in Dehra Dun valued it and Annie good-heartedly wanted to do the right thing for these strangers.

On a whim, she knelt and unwrapped it. Yes, she was certain the jute string was tied differently than the way Karen had tied it weeks ago. It was looser and the knot was different. She laid open the red silk, and there was the odd shapeless stone that she had only seen once before.

She had been told part of its history. It had lain in the earth for unknown centuries before being uncovered by the pickaxe of a tank-digger some time in the nineteenth century. It had been venerated by the Dehra Dun family with sandalwood and sindur, whose colors and coatings were still glued to its surfaces. For a triangle, it was disturbingly irregular along every line. It had both smooth and rough surfaces, as if broken off some larger stone. She and Karen had noted this back in Seattle. It didn't sit straight, no matter how you placed it.

Annie picked it up now and examined it from every angle. It was more isosceles than equilateral. If you held it one way, it looked like a hammer. Held another, it looked like a foot; or a heel, at least. It could be the heel of a sculpture, she thought. And just then she pictured the black Kali from the meditation hall. It could be from something like that, she thought.

She finished her tea. She re-wrapped Shobha's stone in the red silk, winding it tighter. She removed a knot from the jute string, and re-tied it around the red silk, making a double knot just to be sure. She slipped it back in the pillowcase, closed it in the suitcase, shoved it back under the cot, and went to bed.

CHAPTER 18

BRENT

A nnie continued to feel alienated from ashram life, and so she began fitting an afternoon walk up the hill to Lonnie's cafe into her day. Lonnie always greeted her with a "Hey! Annie!", and knew to bring her a latte, even on the hottest afternoon. "Whassup down there?" Lonnie asked, the first time Annie appeared after the famous Jyoti Prasad night. Lonnie sat down opposite her in her familiar way.

"You wouldn't believe it."

"Try me. I've been here long enough to believe anything."

"Well they can certainly believe anything around here."

"I can believe anything AND nothing, I should have said."

"You were right about the Swami and the girls. Something is going on there. You've heard about the night Jyoti Prasad showed up?"

"And did a full prostration in front of the little goddess? Everyone in India has seen the photos."

"Well, no one has seen Jaswanti since then. Except for the public viewing on Tuesday, we couldn't be sure she's even alive."

"Oh, they aren't going to do anything to her. She's a hot property for them right now. They'll be taking real good care of her." Lonnie tapped the tabletop to emphasize: Real. Good. Care.

"Except in total isolation. She has three sisters, who haven't seen or heard a word. They only see her when they can get close enough to touch her toes at her Tuesday audience. Then they exchange fierce eyelocks that seem to convey distress. But what can they do?"

"Hmm."

"She is imprisoned in some back room of the ashram."

"We could put up a poster: 'Free Jaswanti!'"

A few days later, among the scattered long-haired dudes at the various tables were several new figures. One was a young man in the standard loose T-shirt and faded denims, bent over and picking softly at a guitar. He was whiskery with bedhead hair, the kind of guy who comes from privilege and is having fun living in short-term disguise. As Annie observed him and drew this conclusion, she thought, 'Not unlike me.'

Lonnie, appearing with latte in hand, said, "Annie! We've got another American!" Bedhead glanced up. "This is Brent. Brent, Annie. She's down at Bhav Dham Ashram I was telling you about."

Brent looked up, squinted to shake his concentration, and gave a wave. "Hi there, Annie."

"Brent's working on a book. His guitar is just a disguise."

Brent pantomimed pain with a knife-jab to his heart.

"What's your book about?" asked Annie.

"Well, remember the Beatles?" He gave her a second look, and said, "Yeah, I reckon you do. Well, you know they came to Rishikesh in the sixties?"

"Yep. I've heard about it. Is that what your book is about?"

"Well, it's about swamis. But it begins with the Beatles and the maharishi."

"Isn't the trail grown a little cold?"

"You'd be surprise. A lot of old-timers around here remember it all."

Annie thought about the aging renunciants at Bhav Dham Ashram.

"Maybe some of the people I know."

"Could be. Could be," said Brent.

Annie was remembering all the excitement about the Beatles' connection to the transcendental meditation movement and the Maharishi. She recognized that it might have had. . . come to think of it, certainly had had an impact on her interest in India all those years ago. "Where is the Maharishi now?"

"Dead. Just died a few years ago."

"Here in Rishikesh?"

"No. Holland."

"Holland?!"

"Yeah, in a ritsy resort town, Vlodrop. In a former Franciscan monastery."

"No way!"

"Yeah. TM bought the monastery and built their own over-the-top complex on the grounds. Now they are trying to tear the monastery down, but there are some retro Dutch who want to preserve it. So it's only half torn down. He spent his last two years holed up in a couple of rooms, talking to people by video link."

"Have you checked out the ruins of the old ashram? Other side of the river from here."

"Oh, yeah. The beehive-y looking place. Did that first day I got here. Pretty much of a wreck."

Annie had gone in search of the Maharishi's former ashram during her first week, but it was under guard by the Forest Service, up the hillside on the eastern bank, so she gave it up without getting inside.

"Are the stories about the Maharishi making passes at the pretty girls true?" Lonnie asked Brent.

"Oh, yeah. He was a lech. Remember John Lennon's Sexy Sadie?" Brent strummed and sang a not-too-bad line: "'Sexy Sadie, What have you done? You've made a fool of everyone.' That song started out as 'Maharishi, what have you done.' George made him change the name. He wrote it just before he left India, disillusioned."

Lonnie looked at Annie pointedly. "See what I mean?"

"John left India disillusioned?"

"Swamis can't be trusted."

"'Free Jaswanti' signs going up soon." Annie asked Lonnie the thing she was really interested in: "Any news of Erika or Shobha?"

Lonnie shrugged. "So far as I know, they are still up in the mountains. I'd think they'll be showing up before long. When the rains really get started, it's not such a nice place to be hiking."

☆　☆　☆

"Oh, Annie, we are so glad you have come!" exclaimed Gitanjali. "Come in, have tea. We want to talk to you." They pushed Annie into their one chair, the one she had spent a long and uncomfortable night in a few weeks earlier.

Annie examined each face in turn, none as beautiful as Jaswanti's, but youthful and sweet and good, shiny with the baths they had just finished, though no longer as carefree as the day she had met them on the back road into town.

"Have you heard anything from Jaswanti?"

"Annie, yes!"

"She sent us a note."

"However did she do that? What does she say?"

Kunjlata gave Annie a conspiratorial smile, as if to say, We're not telling, but then immediately she told: "Tyagi Ma," she whispered, close to Annie's ear.

"Shh!" said Sharada, glancing at the door.

"At the Tuesday audience, Tyagi Ma helps out on the dais. Brahmananda is in control, but Jaswanti was able to pass a note to Tyagi Ma. And here it is."

Kunjlata read it to her: *Dearest guru-behen, All my love and blessings to you. Always remembering our happy days at Gunapur, which I often re-live. Also the hard trip from Arrah. Now our guru-dev is everything to us. Your sister, Jaswanti.*

"Annie, Jaswanti is very unhappy!"

"You can tell that from that letter?"

"Yes," explained Sharada. "You see, Gunapur was not a happy place, and Jaswanti never went there. It was me! That was the village where they tried to marry me to an awful old man. Instead of staying there, I ran away that very night. And Arrah was the town where we agreed to meet, at the train station, so we could come to Rishikesh, where Gitanjali and Kunjlata had already come. Jaswanti is reminding us of that. She is saying she wants to run away from an old man who they have given her to."

"Jyoti Prasad!" Kunjlata burst out. "We know that! We just do know that. You could tell that night, what was going to happen!"

There was a silence while everyone was trying to imagine what could possibly be a next step. Everyone in the room had run away, so they were relatively experienced, yet there did not seem to be a logical plan in sight. "Do we know where they are keeping her?" Annie asked.

"Yes, we do. Swamiji has his own rooms over there," Kunjlata pointed toward the north end of the ashram, "on the top floor so he can see Ganga Ma coming out of the hills. There are several rooms there where important guests stay, and Jaswanti is in one of those. It has a garden on the roof and there is an elevator where they bring her down to the meditation hall on Tuesdays."

"But we don't know if she ever leaves that room any other time."

"Annie, you have to help us!"

She looked back at those faces, the faces of young women who had already taken their destinies into their own hands, refused the life planned by their parents, refused husbands, fled far from their villages to this safe haven in the lower Himalayas. Where else was there to go? The higher Himalayas?

"Would you leave here?" she asked.

With some reluctance, Gitanjali said, "We are not afraid to leave here. You talk to those women in town, down by Triveni Ghat. The old ones with the hair." She meant the ones with the matted locks, emaciated, tough, living by begging at the temples. "They have been everywhere. You ask them. They have been to every sacred place, in the north, in the south, in the mountains, in the far, far east in Assam, and beyond Assam. We are prepared for this."

"It is a hard life, Annie," Gitanjali said. "But they are free."

When Annie returned to her room, her heart heavy with the weight of these girls' convictions and determination, she saw with dismay that the suitcase under her bed was now pulled out in the center of the room, lying open. The stone, with its red wrapping, was gone.

Brahmananda, who had been waiting for her, appeared in the doorway. She namaste-ed. "Please," she said, " to follow me. Swamiji wishes to see you."

CHAPTER 19

IN-GROUP

S wamiji had a comfortable, and well cooled, private audience room where special visitors were invited to meet with him. Annie had never been among them, and when she entered the room she guessed with relief that she had not been summoned to be interrogated about the stone in her possession as she had feared. There was a small group of guests, most of them Westerners, most of them sitting comfortably cross-legged on the soft floor mattress at the feet of Swamiji. Beside him, looking small and delicate, sat Jaswanti, her face a mask of emptiness. When she saw Annie enter the room, a quick and brief smile broke her mask.

Brahmananda gestured to a spot on the floor, and Annie let herself down into a cross-legged position, something she was now able to do with some grace. Swamiji was talking as she entered, but when he passed his gaze to her, with a brief but meaningful pause, she felt their beckoning intensity. She felt again the desire to hide in the crowd, to keep out of his way. 'Annie, get a grip,' she told herself.

Swamiji was talking about the powers of Devi, who is the Great Goddess, the Mahashakti. She is the creator of the universe, She is the universal mother, she is the source of all life. Is it not true that all humans are born from the womb of a mother? Even the animals are born of mothers. The essence of that life-giving power is *shakti*, and that is what Hindus, and especially *shakt* Hindus, worship. This was not news to anyone sitting there, who were all well read in this tradition, but it was awesome hearing these ideas from the mouth of the famous Swami in whose temple such astonishing manifestations of the Divine Mother had taken place, and at the feet of beautiful Jaswanti, Her embodiment and exemplar.

It was fascinating to watch him talk. What accounted for his charisma? Annie wondered. He spoke plainly about metaphysical ideas, making them seem obvious and real. Maybe notions of cosmic energy and order have an innate appeal to all sentient beings who share the planet and its universal processes of life and death, day and night, sun and moon, summer and winter. Annie thought that might be true, and since most people do not spend much time thinking such thoughts, an opportunity to do so at the feet of an Indian guru prompts sensations of epiphany. Maybe a group of deer or dogs or whales, if they could comprehend his points, might have the same sense of transcendence.

But it was also his ability to forge personal bonds with each individual sitting there through his piercing eye contact and a slightly bemused air of mystery that made people feel he saw right through them. He saw their surface pose and pierced right through the skin, it was said, down through the neurotic cravings and fears and their earned karma, and into their eternal but hopelessly enmeshed soul. His followers, and above all his Western followers, gave themselves to this masterful intrusion. All the karmic crud was nothing but illusion, amusing illusion, to a great soul like the Swami, and they willingly opened themselves to him. This kind of intimacy, like sex, was binding. Once you have experienced that level of intimacy with another person, the relationship is profoundly permanent.

Annie did not want this kind of relationship with the Swami. She had an inner self that was hers alone, no one else invited, thank you. She wished to deflect all invading lazer eyes. Let street-corner cameras watch her face and coat and shoes, let security x-rays check under her dress, so far nothing could see into her soul, and that was how she wanted it. It was okay for these people sitting here to open their souls to him, but that was their trip, not hers.

Nevertheless, she was glad to have come this close to his inner circle, if that is what this was, and to be able to see Jaswanti again. She kept watch on her out of the corner of her eyes. Jaswanti had more liberty to look at Annie. As always, Jaswanti was shrouded in garlands, her loosened black hair spread over her shoulders and back, a thick red tika in the middle of her forehead. She did not seem to be drugged tonight. Her expression, as she gazed at Annie, varied from perfectly still to a barely perceptible smile and even fainter squint. But if this was a signal of some sort, Annie was missing the meaning. Maybe Jaswanti could only be signalling, 'I'm still myself, Jaswanti, sister of Gitanjali, Kunjlata, and Sharada. I haven't disappeared into the Swami and Devi.'

Swami began describing the manifestations that had electrified the ashram in recent months. These manifestations, in turn, had brought people to the ashram, new people who were searching, called to the possibility of cosmic union offered by worship of shakti. There were many forms such worship could take, many levels of consciousness available to diligent practitioners of Devi-*bhakti*. Such practices, or *tapasya*, conferred powers on devotees, powers that could be used for good or for ill. Dangerous powers that needed to be channeled so as not to destroy those around you, as Devi destroyed the evil Mahisasura. Yes, there were powers to destroy evil, but self-destruction was also a possibility. That was why he, Swamiji, was a guide and guru to those who wished to risk going further—as many now were doing, even including some famous people.

There was a murmur from the little group at Swamiji's feet, who knew all about Jyoti Prasad, whose poll numbers were climbing since his well-published worship of Jaswanti. Of course, no one really knew about Prasad's elevation to greater consciousness later that night, much as they would have liked to know. Annie thought Jaswanti shivered slightly at the mention of 'some famous people.'

People come who have dabbled in other methods of achieving power, Swamiji went on, and there are many such dubious methods available in the world. Some of these methods will get you a little way, then stop you cold. Others are acutely dangerous and could blow up in your face. These people come to be led down the true path, which requires diligent tapasya and guidance. Swamiji did not wish to disparage the limited gains of other paths, his only role was to point people in the right direction, the direction in which true cosmic union was possible.

Swamiji now seemed to be talking directly to Annie. Magic was frivolous and unworthy as a spiritual pursuit. Yes, there were superficial siddhas who could cast spells and make chairs lift and shoot beams of fire, but what was the point of such stunts? Where did they get you? Anyway, those are not true siddhas, they have simply got a little bit of power from tapasya which they squander on tricks. There are sorcerers and mages who are not worthy of respect unless they discipline themselves and control their powers. The first step is to submit to a greater power, accept the authority of a gurudev who will guide you, lovingly and with wisdom, along the path.

The small audience began to pick up on the direction of Swamiji's words, glancing around and finally alighting on Annie's reddening face. They were now smiling at her, the recipient of Swamiji's special attention and favor. But who was she? Some celebrity who had come in disguise? A few whispered questions to each other or volunteered suggestions. Annie thought she heard someone whisper 'Jane Fonda.' This just mortified her further.

Swamiji now turned to a small cushion behind him and pulled out an object while saying, "Devi surprised us again, coming in yet another form. The eternal cosmic Mother's most self-revealing form is here," he announced with drama, and triumphantly held up for all to see Shobha's stone, recently and arrogantly copped from Annie's own suitcase in her presumably locked room. Annie gave a little shock of surprise along with the gasps of others. The black triangular stone, encrusted with sindur and sandalwood, was lifted high. Instantly, hands flew together in prayerful namaskar, and it was several minutes before the reverent murmurs died down.

"We are grateful that you have brought this gift to the ashram," he said, beaming his beatific smile at Annie. "You have done well. We can see that you are already far along the path. We welcome you to our community. We rejoice in your progress. Soon, we believe, you will be ready to take *diksha.*" Again that little gasp from the crowd.

With that, Swamiji stood. He received namaskar from the crowd, offered it back, and turned to leave. Brahmananda appeared instantly to help Jaswanti to her feet. With a last, quick questioning glance at Annie, Jaswanti turned away, following Swamiji out of the room.

☆   ☆   ☆

Back in her room, Annie slammed her immersion heater into a mug of water to make herself a cup of tea. Her hands were still shaking with rage, even after walking across the compound to her room, soundly locked as always. Nothing left of interest to rip off, she thought angrily as she had unlocked the door. May as well leave it unlocked after this.

She felt invaded and manipulated. She had been singled out and coerced into submission. She had been mute – or muted? – unable to say a word. Of course, that was his brilliance; what if he had offered her an opportunity to speak? What would she have said? Would she have said, No, not at all, I don't want to be your disciple? Then why was she there, sitting in the inner circle AT HIS FEET?

Could she have said, That's my stone? You stole it from me! Give it back?

Probably not. That's the kind of social coward she was.

And this mage thing had gotten out of hand and turned against her. She never claimed to be a mage. At least, she didn't think she had. He had pulled that out of her, too, by publicly commanding her to come up with a 'vision.' And then people talk, and Tyagi Ma had it in her head the night of Kali's blood and Annie's flashlight beam. How ridiculous was that?

Annie felt she was getting sucked in deeper, and now she had lost control of the stone, and Shobha was nowhere in sight. She had more or less promised to help the sisters spring Jaswanti from her spiritual incarceration, which was not remotely possible. This had turned into an absolute mess.

✵ ✵ ✵

Among the new seekers at Swamiji's private session were Seema and Nic. They had arranged for a quiet meeting with Swamiji earlier in the day, at which they presented themselves as wealthy seekers who had frequented Osho's ashram in Pune, but were searching for something less. . . trendy. While they were admirers of the late Zorba the Buddha, he was gone now, and their feeling was that most of the remaining power of his movement was social and fiscal rather than spiritual. Whereas they had been following the events of Swamiji's ashrams in recent newspaper accounts, and it was their observation that truly miraculous manifestations were taking place here in Rishikesh. They had recently been in Banaras where they visited his small ashram but missed him, and before that in Kamakhya, where they had also missed him; and so they had resolved to finally connect with him at his main ashram in Rishikesh.

From these reports, Swamiji keenly perceived that this couple were serious seekers and potentially important followers. You only had to look at them to know they were wealthy, and the large initial check they presented was additional evidence. He presented them with his own special rudrakshamala, one for each, and invited them back that evening. About their marital situation, he could guess but did not ask. They gratefully declined his offer of two rooms in the ashram – his and hers – saying they already had taken a place nearby.

That was how it happened that they were among the devotees in the room when the gift of Shobha's stone was made public, the donation of an American woman who was sitting among them. Being newcomers, Nic and Seema did not quite follow Swamiji's intriguing words that seemed to point to this woman in some way. Something about acquiring too much magical power from superficial performance of siddhas, and soon to take diksha from him. They both watched her closely, trying to figure out why she was being singled out, why she looked so uncomfortable under Swamiji's attention, what was behind her gift of such a surprisingly rural Hindu object.

It was the object itself that was their main topic of conversation as they walked back up the hill to their small hotel near Lonnie's cafe.

"It's the kind of stone that turns up in fields and tanks and gets set up as village shrines," Seema was saying. "I can't imagine where a middle class American woman would have gotten such a thing."

"It seems to contribute to a sense of Swamiji's movement picking up steam, doesn't it? First our KK, then the little living goddess, now the fieldstone."

"There must be a story there," mused Seema, still thinking about the American.

"Tomorrow I'm getting a close look at KK in the meditation hall," said Nic, thinking about Kamakhya Kali.

CHAPTER 20

MAHAVIDYAS

The next morning, Nic and Seema arrived at the meditation hall early enough to find a nearly empty space. One emaciated old sadhu was sitting against the wall far to the back, winding his turban around his head. From the small heap of possessions around him, it looked like he might have spent the night.

The first thing they did was to sit down close to the front of the room near the images of the gods to do *jap*. Nic worked his way around Swamiji's beads first, because he wasn't actually saying anything, then stood up, leaving Seema sitting there, still actually saying her old mantra. He went close to the shrine, where he made polite namaskar to the gods. Then he allowed himself to fasten his art expert's eye on Kamakhya Kali for the very first time.

She was nearly perfect. He guessed, from her stylistics, she may have been carved in Orissa, probably in the fifteenth century, maybe a century before the Muslim commander Kalapahar came through in 1568. She was four-handed, not uncommon, and easier for sculpture-in-the-round than six, eight, or ten-handed versions. She was in the *pratyalidha* pose, standing on her husband Shiva, holding a sword in an upper hand and a skull in lower one. The other two hands displayed special gestures, the *abhayamudra* and the *varadamudra*. Nic was going to be able to point out to a potential buyer how exquisite the detail work was on the fingers and on the skull. Her tongue, lolling out, wasn't too disgusting. This Kali was delicate and beautiful, in a fearsome way, not ugly as they frequently are. Her waist was slim, her breasts full, her face surprisingly sweet.

The light on the dais was dim, and her feet, both carved as a unit to the prone Shiva, were hard to see. Her right foot was better lighted than the left, and the delicate toes seemed to dig into the flesh of Shiva's stomach. From where he stood, he could hardly tell she was missing a left heel. Too bad about that, but he didn't think it would be a serious impediment when it came to price.

Nic strained to focus on her forehead, where he knew there was a hole going straight through her head. He smiled broadly when he spotted it; well done, he thought. It was carved to look like the famous third eye, an eye that went all the way in—and beyond, through the back wall of the shrine, he assumed, by an assisting tube of some sort. He couldn't get behind to see exactly how it worked.

☆   ☆   ☆

Annie concluded that there was nothing to do but keep doing what she had been doing, despite how furious she was at having been outrageously used by Swamiji, and so with resignation she continued going to Swamiji's morning audiences on the roof, then went to the meditation hall to do jap. She could now go ten times round the beads at one sitting without her mind wandering, although as far as she could tell, without benefit, either. She attended afternoon satsang and evening satsang. At mealtime, she ate her rice and dal with Jaswanti's sisters or else with Tyagi Ma and the widows, then washed her tin plate and cup, and stacked them in the sun along with everyone else's. She continued to be included in the special group at Swamiji's feet most evenings, where she was treated with unfamiliar respect by the other devotees.

The rains were late, and it was nearing July before clouds began to appear in the east, and a few promising sprinkles landed on heads and noses. There was another calendar at work in Annie's head; before long it would be Fourth of July, which India was not planning to celebrate. Lonnie had mentioned to Annie that there was a shady place south of Rishikesh where you could get meat! And beer!

"Really, Annie, you've got to see this place. It's a criminal hangout. You sidle up and whisper, 'fried chicken,' and someone furtively brings you some pieces wrapped in newspaper. You won't get baked beans or potato salad, but chicken and beer is pretty good for Rishikesh."

In this way, Fourth of July became a kind of terminal point, the day she would go 'non-veg,' as they say, again. She would become a wicked meat eater and beer drinker, with no longer any conspicuous virtues to mind.

On the other hand, she could tell she was losing weight on the strictly vegetarian diet, added to the intense heat. She couldn't tell what she looked like, as there were no mirrors to appeal to vanity, but her hip bones had new definition, and if someone guessed she might be Jane Fonda, it seemed like a good sign.

✱   ✱   ✱

One morning in satsang, soon after her addition to Swamiji's late night in-group, Annie noticed a new worshipper, chanting round a rudraksha mala. It was Brent, still with bedhead hair, but now dressed in a long loose T-shirt hanging over a lungi. He was looking gaunt and very much fit in. He was there at evening satsang as well.

There were other newcomers. Ashram regulars had to get there earlier and sit more tightly packed. Swamiji now never missed a night, and seemed more charismatic than ever. Jaswanti continued only to be seen on Tuesdays, but Annie was hearing a new term which seemed to have implications: *Das Mahavidya*. One night after satsang, she and Tyagi Ma sat in Annie's room drinking tea before bed.

"I will never get used to tea without milk and sugar," Tyagi Ma complained, wrinkling her nose. She actually had a tiny refrigerator in her room, which Annie did not, but Tyagi Ma was out of milk.

"You could think of it as a spiritual discipline," Annie suggested, "doing without milk and sugar."

"Some things might be a step too far! I do not seek moksha! I only want my guru and my chai!"

After a bit of chitchat, Annie said, "Tyagi Ma, you have taught me so much, and now I have another question. What does Das Mahavidya mean? I know 'das' is ten, and 'maha' is great."

"And vidya is wisdom. But that alone does not get to the answer to your question. I will explain. The ten mahavidyas are the ten wisdoms, ten incarnations of Devi."

"Ten?!"

"Yes. You see, sakts worship the ten incarnations of Devi, not just one. Or, maybe they have one favorite one, but there are ten in all, and different people chose their favorite, one or another. You see. . . ," there was a special intonation as Tyagi Ma was about to launch into a story, "once Shiva and Parvati got into a quarrel, like any couple can do. They quarreled and quarreled. And Shiva got so mad he threatened to walk out. And Parvati did not like that, and she did not put up with it. Instead, she turned herself into many forms, one after another, ten in all, and each one confronted Shiva. And from each one, he learned a lesson, and that is why they are called the mahavidyas, the 'ten wisdoms.'"

Tyagi Ma sipped her tea, but Annie could tell she was holding something back.

"And so? Why are people talking about das mahavidya right now?"

"Well, some are saying that Jaswanti is Shodashi Tripursundari, the youngest, most beautiful of the mahavidyas. Shodashi means sixteen. A sixteen year old girl is perfection."

"Jaswanti is not sixteen!"

"No, maybe she is a little older than that," Tyagi Ma conceded.

"Is Swamiji looking for other mahavidyas?" Annie's voice came out shocked and stern.

This notion in turn shocked Tyagi Ma. "It is not for him to look. It is for them to reveal."

Annie tilted her head, and said, "Tyagi Ma. You must tell me. What would happen if another great man like Jyoti Prasad came to Swamiji wishing to honor Devi."

"He could worship her image. He could worship Jaswanti."

"But Jyoti Prasad has become famous for Jaswanti. His name is attached to her. Is there not a 'special relationship' there? I think you know what I mean."

Tyagi Ma looked over her shoulder as if to see whether Brahmananda stood in the doorway. "There could be," she said evasively.

"Is it not true that great men sometimes seek to find. . . ," Annie searched for the right way to put this, "spiritual fulfillment with a . . . 'wisdom'."

Tyagi Ma only nodded.

"And would a man such as Jyoti Prasad share his 'wisdom' with another great man? Like, another politician?"

Cornered, Tyagi Ma resisted another minute or two before admitting what Annie was after. There was another long pause while she was making up her mind. Then she began to tell what she knew in a whisper.

"There is a very rich man, not a politician, but a powerful and rich man, who has become Swamiji's disciple. He was very convinced by Jyoti Prasad's link to Jaswanti, and he wanted to experience this same thing. He is a friend of Prasad's, so he must have heard. . . how it went."

Annie had not seen any more big cars pulled up at the back gate, but she could well imagine the flurry of activity, the rush to sweep the great man inside, the fawning, the namaskaring, the flattering little sermons, the presentation of the newest 'vidya.'

"Also," Tyagi Ma added as an afterthought, "there is much money for the ashram. . . . ." She trailed off.

"I'll bet there is. And do you see, this could go on for ten times? Ten rich men, ten mahavidyas? A very good thing for Swamiji's reputation and for the ashram?"

Tyagi Ma nodded. "Formerly, we just worshipped Lord Krishna," she said, almost a whine. "Things were simpler then."

"If Jaswanti is Shodashi Tripursundari, then where is Swamiji going to get nine more? Obviously, they have to be young and beautiful. People like you and me are not at risk."

Tyagi Ma winced at Annie's skepticism.

"Perhaps not. Although Dhumawati was a widow. That was another of the mahavidyas."

"He'd have to find a young widow. And beautiful. Not that easy, maybe."

"Dhumawati swallowed Shiva, her husband, that's how she became a widow." Annie laughed.

"Chinnamasta cut off her own head!" Tyagi Ma was getting into the swing of it. "Who is going to want that?" she giggled.

"Tyagi Ma, do you think this is a good thing?" Annie asked soberly, leaning forward. "Is this good for these girls? Is this good for Jaswanti?"

Tyagi Ma had been pushed as far as she could go this night. "Whether it is good or bad, who can say? Can I question my Gurudev?" She sounded miserable.

The next night, Tyagi Ma appeared at Annie's doorway looking excited, face glistening with the evening heat. She glanced back down the hall, entered Annie's room, and shut the door behind her. Annie was stretched out on the bed with the book on Hindu asceticism propped on her stomach, but it was too hot to concentrate or to sleep.

"Annie!"

She put the book down and sat up.

"Annie, news. There is a new vidya!"

"There is? Who?"

"Gauri!" Tyagi Ma sat down at the foot of Annie's bed and pulled a leaf fan out of her sari. "Oof, it is so hot!"

"Is that one of the mahavidyas?" She had been reading about them and was trying to memorize the ten names. She didn't remember Gauri.

"No, Gauri is one of the nine avatars of Durga."

"Nine?! On top of the ten mahavidyas?!"

"Yes, Gauri married Shiva. She was a very lucky goddess to get such a good husband. Young girls in my place pray to her. But here is what I have just learned. Jyoti Prasad's rich friend is to have Gauri. Tomorrow night he comes."

"Oh! My! But who?"

"Here is what you must know. Gauri is called 'the golden one.' That is what everyone knows about this goddess. So who do you think?"

"Tell me."

"The German girl!"

"Oh, surely not! She just came here. She's brand new. What does she know about all this?"

"What she knows, I do not know. Brahmananda will take care of that."

"How do you know all this? From Brahmananda?"

"Well. . . ," Tyagi Ma began. "I listen, I see things. This is MY wisdom, my vidya." She put her finger over her lips and smiled conspiratorially. "Brahmananda is in charge of these things. Some may not like her so much. . . ." Annie had observed that Tyagi Ma herself did not like Brahmananda very much. "But Swamiji depends on her and listens to her advice. This morning they were talking about P.N. Maharaj, the friend of Jyoti Prasad. He will have the special room when he comes, they were saying. Actually there are two rooms, one for sleeping, one for prayer." Tyagi Ma paused to be sure Annie understood her. "You understand? Then Swamiji said, 'You will prepare Katrin.'"

Annie was thinking about the young blond German girl at her very first audience on the rooftop with Swamiji. He gave her rudrakshamala and encouraged her to do *jap*. That was Katrin's first day, too. How could they be thinking of subjecting her to this so soon? Or was the girl more cosmopolitan than she had seemed? Annie hadn't made any effort to get to know her. She saw her frequently enough, at satsang, at meals, but there was a reserve about Katrin that kept Annie at a distance. She was now regretting it.

Annie appreciated that she was now being incorporated into the gossip circle of the older women of the ashram, who up to now had given her little more than aloof nods when she was near. Or at least, there was a single loose mouth in that circle that whispered its secrets to her. Brahmananda wasn't going to confide in her any time soon. Annie wondered how much she dared risk with Tyagi Ma. She decided to try her luck.

"Tyagi Ma, do you know of a young woman named Shobha?"

Tyagi Ma's eyes widened. "Shobha?"

"You must have heard of her. She was at this ashram, I think."

"Yes, she was. She isn't here any more."

"So I gather. But why not?"

"I'm not certain. There was some issue. You shouldn't ask about her."

"Is she someone Brahmananda would know more about?"

"Brahmananda knows about everything. But I wouldn't ask her if I were you. It might be a touchy subject," she ended vaguely.

"Was she a vidya?"

"All I know is that she was a beautiful, very sincere young women. Very devout. Gurudev favored her very much. Then she left. I do not know more than that."

"When did she go? How long ago?"

"It was in the spring, before the heat. Maybe in April sometime. I can't tell you more than that."

"Thank you, Tyagi Ma. You have been a good friend to me."

Tyagi Ma beamed and fanned.

CHAPTER 21

GAURI

On the first day of July, black clouds appeared over the eastern hills, and by mid-morning big wet drops were splattering the softened asphalt of the hot roads of Rishikesh. The temperature dropped ten degrees in as many minutes, and people rushed into the open to feel the rain on their heads and faces. Vikram drivers beeped their horns in delight, and the sound of rain hitting dry leaves and wheels splashing wet streets was added to the soundtrack of life at riverside.

No one was more thrilled than Annie, a native child of rain. As the sky opened she was making her way to Dr. Gupta's clinic, and she was joyfully soaked by the time she arrived. There, even the doleful mothers were perked up, and children were busy stomping in mud puddles.

Jayanti Gupta was saying, "Yes, yes, bring her in right now" to her nurse as Annie appeared in the doorway. She waved Annie in. "Annie! Sit. Tell me all the latest." To the nurse: "Shut the door please. Don't disturb us." She pulled off her glasses to listen better, and patted the bun at the back of her head. "What a relief, this rain at last!"

"Yes! Glorious rain."

"Do you know, the rains in our culture are associated with romantic passion. Radha goes to her lover, Krishna, as the monsoons swell. In Bollywood films, you have dancing in wet saris. Even ascetic ashrams may not be impervious, I understand." She stopped and pushed her head forward as if to say, Am I not right?

"Have you heard about P. N. Maharaj?"

"Is THAT who it is!"

"You HAVE heard."

"Well, I've heard rumors that another Big Man is on the line. Big money this time."

Annie wondered about her sources, but was relieved that she wasn't the only leak from the ashram.

"There's going to be no end to this. I've just heard about the ten mahavidyas and the nine Durgas."

Dr. Gupta laughed. "Never underestimate Hindu mythology. It is endlessly inventive. Anything is possible."

"Jaswanti is, apparently, Shodashi Tripursundari. And now they have a Gauri. A young German girl who came about the same time I did. Lovely blonde, blue eyes. I don't really know her."

"No, I haven't heard about her. Will she accept the role, I wonder. These ideas aren't part of her culture." Dr. Gupta refrained from remarks about the foolishness of Westerners who come around looking for spiritual adventures that they never understand. Or the corrupting influence that has on local people.

"If they drug her, that may be all it takes to put her in a passive state." Annie had experience of this from her own youth; a short period of drug-soaked great sex that she sometimes looked back on with wonder. Would there be a public presentation as there had been for Jaswanti? "There is going to be no end to this. Swamiji is really on a roll."

"Yes. All the publicity is making him famous and these powerful supporters will protect him," Dr. Gupta said, but Annie wondered whether they wouldn't quietly disappear if things went bad.

Jaswanti's sisters want to rescue her and get away."

"Do they," she nodded thoughtfully, then shook her head. "I don't doubt it, but that won't be easy. They lock the ashram every night, and there are eyes everywhere."

Annie described her conversations with the sisters, their declaration that they wanted only freedom, they were willing to be homeless like the begging sadvi down at Triveni Ghat. Dr. Gupta shook her head and laughed softly.

"That is not as easy a life as they think. You should talk to those women, Annie. They have had very hard lives. Many of them have been abandoned by their husbands, or their husbands are dead, or their children kicked them out in their old age. They are easily taken advantage of by the male sadhus, who are not all as holy as they seem. Although if they travel in groups, they are safer."

"Well the first task is to get Jaswanti away, and then the four of them need someplace to go. I thought you might have some ideas about that."

"Oh my. Let me think." She thought. "Of course, they could come here as a first step. I could keep them for a little while. There are many, many other ashrams where women are safe. In Haridwar, for instance. Some of them require endowments from their families. And there are many more in Vrindavan."

She reminded Annie that she was not on good terms with the ashram, and Annie remembered how she had hidden her face on the day she visited Jaswanti, and tried to leave unseen. This was because she had been an outspoken critic of the ashram for years; it did not provide medical care when its ordinary members got sick, although Swamiji and his main aides got good medical treatment; not from her, of course. A few years ago one of the widows had sickened with dysentery, and when they finally carried her down the hill to the clinic, she was past saving. "And we had the expense of burning her body," she added. There were other incidents, no need to go into them, but she was no fan of Swamiji or his ashram.

Would Swamiji allow them to leave? Annie wondered. Could they just inform him they want to go, for instance? Dr. Gupta doubted it would be so simple. They had taken *diksha* from him; he was their gurudev for all time. It was like a marriage that couldn't be ended. Not that some didn't end, but there would be resistance. Especially now with the spotlight on the ashram, fleeing devotees would not be a good addition to the story that was being nurtured in the media. And even if the three sisters could get away, it would be much, much more difficult for Jaswanti.

As Annie trudged back up the hill, her sandals slapping on the wet pavement and rivulets trickling down her back and arms, she pondered ways to get the four girls out of the ashram. Even if that proved possible, what about herself, once they were gone? She wasn't going to leave Shobha's stone with Swamiji. It had been safe, after all, at Karen's house back in the states. She had brought it back to India, only to have it end up in the hands of the very person it was probably being protected from in the first place. She had made things worse, not better. She felt incompetent. She was an incompetent troublemaker, as unable to control her life now as she had been at home with Ted. The only difference was now she was making things worse for other people. If she could find a way to help the four sisters, that would change something in the world. Getting the stone back from Swamiji seemed even more impossible, and where was Shobha anyway? How did Shobha think Karen could get the stone back to her when she was going to disappear?

✻ ✻ ✻

At satsang that night, Annie was alert for any evidence of another important personage showing up to worship Kali, or revelation of a new incarnation, but there was no hint of anything exceptional. She saw no sign of Katrin. She did see Brent, working away on his beads against a far wall.

After satsang, she joined the in-group in Swamiji's private chamber. Eight or ten of the group were European devotees, several married couples who she sensed were trying to appear chaste, and a number of middle aged singles, several men with fraying beards and creased cheeks, and one heavy woman with thin hair pulled back into an unattractive brown bun. Most of them were wearing white shawls over versions of Indian clothing. There was a rather attractive couple, a tall blond Western man with a strikingly beautiful Indian woman, who were becoming permanent members of this group. Annie did not feel like one of this group, but here she was, a fraudulent mage in her own version of Indian clothing, her hair still damp from its earlier soaking.

In addition to the Europeans, there were several Indians that Annie hadn't seen before. One portly gentleman, possibly in his late fifties, with a thin fringe of hair glued across the top of his scalp, was looking uncomfortable in the lotus position. He wore a white kurta and dhoti and a Rolex watch. Annie could guess who this was. Two younger men sat beside him. At one point, the older man glanced at his watch, and leaned over to whisper something to one of the young men, who immediately left the room.

Then Swamiji entered, followed by Jaswanti followed by Brahmananda and Narayan in the usual procession. Swamiji beamed at the little group, did a deep and unusually warm namaste in answer to their folded hands. His eyes were shining, and he actually made a little joke:

"Ganga Ma is falling to earth again!" Everyone knew the mythology of the Ganges falling out of the heavens and being caught in Shiva's matted locks – his *kesh* – after which Rishikesh was named. The group laughed in appreciation of the myth and the joke and the rain that had finally arrived. He seated himself comfortably on his cushion, while Brahmananda helped Jaswanti to sit beside him to his right. Usually she was at his left, but tonight there was a spare cushion in Jaswanti's usual place.

Swamiji began by welcoming his old and new friends, commending their devotion and spiritual discipline. He praised Devi, the Mahashakti, the Creatrix of the Universe, who had bestowed special favor on their ashram. He was humbled at this favor, he himself desired only to know her, to serve her, to experience her, to show the way to her. He did not seek fame or wealth. This was the most difficult of paths, because it involved rituals that could be misused, that could be abused, that could overwhelm the practitioner. The typical ignorant person, mired in *maya*, would not understand that forbidden items could be used to transcend dualism into cosmic unity. They would see forbidden items as goals in themselves, falling deeper into ignorance. Only the true siddha dared follow this path. Woe to the person who attempted this path without proper training and self-discipline.

Deviji continued to *rain* – he paused for his pun to be appreciated – blessings on the ashram. Her visitations continued to astonish him. Of course, Devi was naturally within all women to some degree, but she could also make her abode in special women, taking possession of them and making her presence known by certain signs. Sometimes these signs were esoteric, so that only a siddha could identify them; at others, even a small child would understand that THERE is Devi! Such was, again, the astonishing situation at the ashram.

He paused at length for effect. Did the lights dim? It seemed so. People glanced at each other in surprise. A bit of incense floated on the breeze stirred by the overhead fan. The side door opened, but for a moment no one appeared. Everyone clearly heard some murmured resistance, but then Brahmananda entered, leading Katrin, the German girl, forward. She was wearing a glittering golden sari, evidently heavy, for she walked uncertainly and Brahmananda had to help lift the skirt, which Katrin kept stumbling on. Katrin seemed confused as she was led to the cushion and made to sit down on it. She looked frightened. Her blonde hair was brushed forward across her chest, and garlands of golden tinsel circled her neck. Once Brahmananda got her seated, she retreated backward into the shadow, keeping a concerned eye on her newest Devi.

The little group of devotees at Swamiji's feet may not have given quite the reaction he was expecting. They seemed, if anything, puzzled. No one really could imagine a Hindu goddess looking like this. Jaswanti was more what they expected. Annie kept looking back and forth at the two goddesses flanking Swamiji. Katrin's eyes were empty and she could barely keep them open. Jaswanti's were alert, watching the audience carefully. There was the faintest of smirks on her lips.

Swamiji continued with a little sermon explaining how Devi had made herself known in Katrin. Katrin's *jap* had proceeded with astonishing accomplishment. At kirtan, she attained a state of *bhav* not seen in many a life-long devotee. Once last week the bhav was so deep they became alarmed, and tried to shake her out of it. 'Why do you disturb me?' asked a voice that was not Katrin's. 'Leave me be. I am Gauri, you do not know me.'

The audience gasped at this and looked hard at Katrin. She seemed to tip sideways, and Brahmananda rushed to set her straight again. As Swamiji continued, Katrin closed her eyes altogether and toppled over backward.

At this there was serious alarm. Swamiji turned to look closely at Katrin. Katrin was not responsive. He motioned to Brahmananda, making a firm gesture toward the side door. Brahmananda tried to get Katrin to stand, but Katrin was beyond standing. Narayan rushed up, and so did the remaining assistant to P. N. Maharaj. The three of them helped the limp goddess out of the room and into the darkened side room.

Swamiji turned back to his audience, but seemed rattled. He attempted an explanation: the girl, being a foreigner, perhaps did not have adequate preparation for possession by this great divinity. If this was his fault, he regretted it. His sole purpose is to honor Devi and lead others to her. They had just had a demonstration of how powerful this goddess is, which he was sure none of them would ever forget. It was a great privilege to see the visible workings of the Great Goddess. Jai Shakti!

With that he rose and departed. Jaswanti, too, stood up, shook her skirt, and followed him out.

✵ ✵ ✵

As they were being ushered out of Swamiji's special audience room, the little group of Western devotees milled in the courtyard, wondering about what they had just seen. "Who was that girl?" one of the men asked, evidently British.

"That is Katrin, from Germany," Annie said.

"Oh, are you staying here at the ashram?" asked the man's wife.

"Yes," said Annie. Instantly she became the expert on what was going on. The others, including Seema and Nic, gathered around her.

"She was in a rather advanced state of bhav, wasn't she?" the man's wife said.

"She was drugged," said Annie. The woman gasped. "They overdosed her on bhang."

"The other girl didn't seem to be drugged," observed her husband.

"No, but she was the night Jyoti Prasad was here."

"Were you here then?" he asked.

"I was here," Annie nodded. "Tonight I think we had another important person."

"Who was it? I didn't recognize him," said the wife.

"I did," said Seema. "That's P. N. Maharaj, a very rich, very powerful businessman."

"Well, what's going on then?"

"They get a special audience with the girl," Annie said. "Very special."

The British couple looked at each other.

"I mean, what do you think Tantra is all about?" Annie said with irritation. "It's probably going on right now. Poor Katrin."

Nic and Seema left the little group to walk back to their hotel. Nic was worrying about his KK, with someone like Maharaj around. He knew this man's investing habits. He was a crass collector, investing in art as a place to store money. On the other hand, if he was a dabbler in Tantra, an image like KK would have extra meaning to him, a bonus of social capital. But he couldn't be expected to buy it out from under his gurudev, if that's what the swami was to him. In fact, it was not convenient for Nic that Maharaj had first hand knowledge of the connection between KK, which Nic was soon to take off into the art investor world, and this swami. He could imagine a scene where a Bombay magnate shows off his new acquisition at a party, and one of the guests, who happens to be this Maharaj, exclaims, 'That's my gurudev's Kali!'

Seema was thinking about Katrin. It bothered her that the German girl was obviously very young and out of her depth. What was Swamiji thinking? One might think it was exploitive of him, taking an inexperienced girl like this, not even really a Hindu, whatever her interests in Hinduism might be, and setting her up as a Kali avatar. Seema's experience of swamis was wide-ranging, she accepted them as a natural part of her Hindu world, and she respected her own family's gurudev. But there were unscrupulous ones, and now she was wondering about this Rishikesh swami. Using a young innocent, exotic thing like Katrin to hook in the likes of Maharaj!

The girl should not have been drugged. Of course Tantrics all use bhang and ganja, everyone knows that, but to drug this girl and then let Maharaj have his little puja with her later on – that ugly man! – was indefensible.

CHAPTER 22

_____ MIDNIGHT _____

On the uphill side of the ashram there is a rocky ledge within the ashram grounds reached by a paved walk from behind the Meditation Hall. At its end, high up over the rear courtyard, is a stone bench under a deodar where one can sit and watch the comings and goings through the back gate. This is where Annie found herself after the scene in the private audience. She was too agitated to return to her room, and she would have liked to walk down along the river, but she knew the main gate would be locked. Instead, she came to the crow's nest, as it was called, to clear her head.

That is how she saw the next phase of Swamiji's courting of fame and fortune unfold. A silver Mercedes was parked in the courtyard, its driver standing by the open rear door. Before long, the back ashram door opened, and P. N. Maharaj hurried out to his car, his two assistants trailing him. One hopped into the back seat beside him while the other waved orders to someone to open the back gate. A servant rushed to unlock it and pull the gate inward. As the second assistant jumped into the front passenger seat, the Mercedes zoomed backward out the gate, swung around, and headed off downhill. The gate clanged shut.

Annie observed that Maharaj was leaving in a big hurry. She checked her watch, and saw that it was only forty-five minutes since the audience had ended. What had been going on? She didn't have a clear idea what these rich guys were doing with their little goddesses, but she had some guesses, and it didn't seem like whatever it was could be done with any elegance in so short a time. Particularly when the object of it all was drugged out of her mind and surely had to be brought around. But maybe not. Maybe unconscious was good enough. Who could she ask?

As she was wondering about this, the back door opened again. This time it was Narayan. He walked out into the courtyard and looked around. Annie backed into the shadow of the deodar, pulling the edge of her sari down over her face, and tried not to move. But Narayan wasn't checking for observers. Someone was coming up the road. The gate opened again, and two bearers carrying a stretcher entered the courtyard and set it down. There they squatted silently while Narayan went back inside. One of them lighted a bidi, and soon the acrid smoke was drifting up to Annie.

Narayan reappeared and motioned to the two men to come inside. The smoker flicked his bidi away, and followed him. In a few minutes they reappeared, carrying a body. It was fully wrapped in layers of white and saffron cloth, so that it was impossible to identify the corpse. The men tied twine around the body and the stretcher, Narayan flicked some flowers onto it in a perfunctory way, they hoisted it and set off through the gate and down the road. Within a minute the courtyard was empty again.

Annie sat mutely, stunned by what she had seen.

Katrin had come to Swamiji's ashram for healing. She was just nineteen when her mother's breast cancer was diagnosed, and as it was slowly killing her, her mother tried to prepare her to cope with her death. They lived in a village not far from Munich, where Liz had settled with her German boyfriend at the end of her hippie years, traded weed for good German wines, and tried to live according to the Maharishi's core principles while also embracing middle class German life. She had come from London to Rishikesh in the early seventies looking for whatever it was that had inspired the Beatles, stayed for several years, and met Gunnar. Eventually Gunnar grew bored with the Rishikesh scene and wanted to go back to Germany, finish his education and have a real career. Liz went with him.

Katrin came along shortly before Liz's biological clock expired, at the age of forty, a delightful surprise after years of reproductive failure. Liz sold her popular English Tea Shoppe in order to devote herself to raising Katrin. Liz saw that Katrin had inherited her blonde good looks from her father, and something less desirable from herself, a tendency toward darkness and depression that could last for weeks, until a 'mood' passed and her nature turned sunny again. Liz used the meditation techniques she had learned from the Maharishi to control her mood swings, and tried to teach these stabilizing methods to Katrin.

During her teen years, Katrin loved to hear stories from her mother's 'hippie days,' and Rishikesh became for her as mythological a place as it actually was in Hindu lore. She knew all the stories. . . of Ganga's fall from Heaven into Shiva's hair, of the holy places further north, including the 'Cow's Mouth,' Gaumukh, the source of the Ganges at an opening in Himalayan rock. When her mother died, she knew she had to come here to find, in a sense, her mother's soul, and also her own.

Her father agreed to fund the trip, and Katrin spent a great deal of time on the internet, researching ashrams, locating them on Google Earth, and emailing bloggers who wrote about their experiences in Rishikesh. In this way, she found Bhav Dham Ashram and Swamiji.

Katrin was delighted in her quiet way to be so warmly received by the Swami, and longed to please him by excelling at all the disciplines he taught, many of which she had also learned from her mother. Swamiji would invite her to private sessions with him, in which he encouraged her to talk about her German back ground. He was hoping to enlarge his following among Europeans, and felt a need to know more about these exotic others, who had left their own religion behind and were coming to India to replace it. This daughter of a woman who had been a follower of the Maharishi was an especially valuable find. The Maharishi had died, it was said, a billionaire. He had long ago abandoned his Rishikesh ashram to the forest, while building a newer, finer one someplace near Germany, where he lived into a revered and luxurious old age. Swamiji thought if the Maharishi could do this, so could he.

Shortly after Jaswanti was 'discovered,' Swamiji summoned Katrin to inform her that her spiritual progress was so exceptional that she deserved to be moved to special quarters reserved for, as he put it, prodigies. Katrin, who had always been treated as a special child, just smiled and accepted the tributes Swamiji bestowed on her. Brahmananda, in her fawning way, patted her and helped her pack her few things, and personally carried them into the main building and up the elevator to the air conditioned rooms of the well-favored. Her new room was still ascetic, with only a bed, a chair, and a table, but it had a window overlooking the upper Ganges. She loved this room; the scene outside the window reminded her of her

Bavarian homeland. Late at night she would crank open the window and allow a cooling natural breeze from the north to fill her room. She would sit at her desk and fill her journal with her thoughts, her longing for her mother, her growing affection for Swamiji, the serenity of her daily spiritual life, the beauty of the environment.

Next door to her was the mysterious Jaswanti, powerfully charged with the presence of the goddess. Katrin was in awe of her, and yet, in almost every way she could detect, Jaswanti seemed like an ordinary young woman. Jaswanti had appeared to be as delighted when Katrin moved in next door as would any solitary young woman who finally had a friendly neighbor to talk to. Jaswanti took her down the short hall to a terrace open to the heavens, filled with boxed trees and climbing bougainvillea over a pergola at one end. From this elevated garden, they were prevented by high walls from seeing down into the grounds of the ashram, but they could see the treetops, the distant hills, and the sky. Here they sat and talked during the few hours of the day not taken up by private jap, kirtan, satsang, and meditation in the presence of Swamiji.

Katrin was longing to know what it felt like to Jaswanti to have the goddess dwelling inside her, but she couldn't make the questions come out. Instead, she posed these questions in her journal: "Does it feel like a divine presence inside your actual body? Is it physical, does it glow or flutter? Does she feel separate from you? Do you actually have supernatural powers? Can you leave your body? Is Kali a separate personality inside your head? Can you think Kali's memories? Are you sometimes her and sometimes yourself? When you are in bhav, are you aware of what is going on outside yourself?"

The morning the rains started, Katrin was doing *jap* under the pergola in the rooftop garden when Swamiji came up behind her in his silent way. He wanted to talk about the next step in her training. She had been moving forward in great strides, he said, and he thought she was ready for a special initiation. She had already taken diksha from him, receiving his mantra and several tokens of his affection for her, including a new rudrakshamala and saffron robe. He had waived the usual lifetime membership fees in light of her special status. The new initiation would happen soon, perhaps as early as this evening, and Brahmananda would spend the day in preparing her for it. But he had to be sure she was willing to accept this path and trust in his guidance. Katrin nodded, eyes wide and glistening. He patted her head, nodding in benign, ambiguous, and tender approval.

Greatly excited, Katrin went directly to her journal, describing this conversation with every detail she could remember. While she was doing this, Jaswanti knocked on her door and let herself in. She sat on Katrin's bed and watched her write.

"Just let me finish this, and I will tell you," Katrin said, still breathless. When she put down her pen, she turned to Jaswanti. "Guess what? Tonight I am to have a special diksha."

Jaswanti's mouth dropped open and her face paled. "No, Katrin," she said.

"What?"

"Don't. Don't do it. You mustn't."

At that moment, the door opened and Brahmananda entered, carrying a tray and some packages wrapped in brown paper. Jaswanti turned to look at Brahmananda with something like fear.

"Making conversation here, are we?" Brahmananda said sternly. She stooped to set her burden down on the bed, and straightened up, putting her hands on her hips to address Jaswanti. "Katrin is busy now."

Jaswanti looked back at Katrin with wide, warning eyes, as she left the room.

Brahmananda's demeanor turned soothing and deferential. "Tonight is special night for you," she said. "Today, we make ready." Katrin was not used to the kind of personal ministrations she had been getting since coming to her special room. Each day, Brahmananda oversaw her bath, which consisted of taking her into the little private bathroom, helping her remove her sari, petticoat, and choli, and ladling cold water over her body, starting with the top of her head. She handed her soap so Katrin could do the detail work, but Brahmananda supervised it all. Katrin no longer had to wash her own sari and find a shrub to lay it over to dry. This day, Katrin got special treatment. She was seated on a low stool, so that Brahmananda could shampoo her hair. Afterward, Brahmananda produced a bottle of oil that she intended to pour into her hair, but Katrin objected. "No oil!"

"Yes, oil," Brahmananda insisted.

"You don't understand my kind of hair," Katrin insisted. Brahmananda shrugged and gave it up. Wielding a narrow-toothed comb, she spent a long time combing the tangles out of Katrin's hair until it was smooth and shiny and almost dry.

When it came time to dress, Brahmananda opened one of the brown paper packages. Rather than another cotton saffron-colored sari, which was what Katrin was expecting, there was a sari glittering in gold-threaded ornamentation. Brahmananda cooed in admiration; clearly she hadn't seen it until now. She lifted a corner of it, as if to weigh it. 'Heavy,' she murmured. She opened the second package, which contained a veil of gold chiffon heavily embroidered in gold thread. Katrin reached to touch the veil, running her hand over its rich surface.

"Why?" Katrin asked, puzzled. "Why so beautiful?" She could not understand what this sari had to do with her vow of simplicity and poverty.

"A gift to Gauri," replied Brahmananda.

Brahmananda turned from the glittering cloth to the pale naked girl. She handed her the petticoat, and ordered, "Put on." Katrin stepped into it, pulled it up around her hips, and tied the string tightly. "Now choli." The high-waisted blouse, made of the same fabric as the sari, went on next.

"No bra?"

"No need."

All business, Brahmananda went about wrapping the sari around the petticoat, tucking it in, twisting the front pleats in expert motions, shaking it to check the fall, tucked the folds into the front of the petticoat. The rest of the sari wrapped around again, came up over the choli from from front to back over Katrin's left shoulder. On second thought, she brought the edge over her shoulder from back to front and spread it over her torso so that the unique edge was visible across her chest.

The next hour was spent on make-up, hair, gold ornaments, and arrangement of the veil to make the most of Katrin's beautiful white-blonde hair. She submitted dumbly, always a little afraid of Brahmananda, and insecure about Hindu customs, which she feared to offend.

By evening, all was complete. Brahmananda left the room to inform Swamiji, leaving Katrin alone in her heavy robes and her empty thoughts. Soon after Brahmananda left, the door opened softly and Jaswanti entered.

"Wah!" she exclaimed softly. "You look beautiful." Jaswanti looked beautiful, too, wearing the clothing she wore for her audiences as Shodashi Tripursundari.

"But what is it about?" Katrin asked. "Why have they dressed me like this?"

Jaswanti had immediately understood. She had seen events unfolding around Katrin that were identical to events that had enveloped her. She was certain there was no escape. Although the doors to their rooms were usually unlocked, the entire wing of the building was always locked and always guarded. Swamiji, Brahmananda, and Narayan had the keys.

"Katrin, you are the new Devi. That is what they are saying."

Katrin opened her mouth to speak, but no words came out.

Jaswanti leaned forward to be closer to Katrin's face. "They will give you bhang, which you must drink. This will make it easier to bear."

"What? No," she whispered.

"I have tried to escape. There is no escape. The bhang will help."

"What will happen?"

"There will be a ceremony. They will worship you."

"Why do I need bhang for that?'

"At the end, you will not like it."

It was past midnight when Annie finally decided on a plan. She had thought through a number of alternatives, all risky, some ridiculous, most likely to fail. Nor were chances good for the plan she was now embarked on, but sometimes in life one has to be proactive.

The first thing she did, back in her room, was rummage through the suitcase under the bed. She checked her iPhone; totally dead. Anyway, there was never a signal here. Then her laptop: near death. It lived long enough for her to type a description of what she had seen tonight. Just in case.

The next thing she did was knock on Tyagi Ma's door.

☆   ☆   ☆

CHAPTER 23

_____ ANOTHER DREAM _____

Swamiji was in a state of utter unmindfulness; in fact, of full out agitation. The day had been perfectly stage-managed. No one could have guessed that it could go so badly wrong. His new devotee, referred to him by Jyoti Prasad, had arrived in the early afternoon according to plan. They had met, talked, and Swamiji had offered a simple vegetarian meal on a thali served on the upper verandah, overseeing while Maharaj ate alone. Swamiji had impressed him with stories of Kali's manifestations over the last year, some of which Maharaj had already heard, but he was clearly enjoying all the insider details. "Ahh!" he'd say, "*Achcha!*"

The evening plans did not include a grand public presentation of Gauri, with Maharaj prostrating himself before her. He was not a politician; he was the opposite of politicians. He avoided publicity rather than seeking it. Understanding this, Swamiji had leaked news of a new avatar in the form of Gauri, allowing rumor to spread, but he did not present her at satsang. Nor was Maharaj in attendance. Maharaj always worked behind the scenes, in private, negotiating, working deals, pressuring opponents, building a small empire in luxury goods catering to India's rising middle class. The sari presented to Katrin came from one of his most prestigious outlets, where saris sold for *lakhs* of rupees and Bollywood starlets came to shop.

Maharaj had built this empire from a small shop he had inherited from his father and uncle close to Connaught Place in Delhi. Every morning he lighted incense to Devi as his father had done before him. He welcomed lady shoppers as if they were Devi incarnate, as he tried to think of them and often joked: "All women are Deviji, *hai na?*" he'd say. Large matrons sometimes were annoyed by this, but he was certain that underneath they welcomed the flattery, and he thought it helped sales.

The fact was, he believed it all. He was from a community that slaughtered a goat every year at Durga Puja, and believed that a year without the offering would be a year of business failure. He took no chances. As a devout Hindu, he had donated to Jyoti Prasad's Hindutva party before anybody even knew the name of Jyoti Prasad. During the campaigns over the Babri Mosque, he had donated enough bricks to build the entire Ram Temple. Of course, the temple was never built, though they got rid of the mosque, and most of the money went to support the Ram Temple campaign, and later Jyoti Prasad's campaign for Lok Sabha. Since then they had become fast friends, often eating together even though they were from different castes (Prasad was lower, and technically Maharaj shouldn't be eating with him at all, ever).

After all the publicity over Prasad and Shodashi Tripursundari, Maharaj had called him up. He got Prasad to tell him all about his tantric adventure, and then asked Prasad for an introduction to Swamiji.

All seemed to be going well during the private viewing of Gauri at sunset. While Maharaj had a little rest, servants cleaned the spot under the vine-draped trellis where Maharaj had eaten and gave it a purifying coat of cowdung. They had set out a low stool, and brought Katrin out, stumbling over the heavy sari which Brahmananda had to keep lifting for her. They got her seated on the stool, arranged the folds of rich fabric, and photographed her. Swamiji then approached her in deep reverence (without prostration), offered flowers and lighted a *diya*.

When Maharaj joined them, looking fresh from a bath, Swamiji could not miss an expression of repugnance on Katrin's face. Swamiji did not have enough wisdom about gender to grasp that a beautiful young woman like Katrin might have an aversion to a man such as Maharaj. Where Swamiji saw an immensely rich and powerful wheeler dealer, who would enrich his ashram and enhance his own prestige, Katrin saw an old fat man with round bulging eyes and a waddle. Maharaj did not sense that, either. He grinned, namaste-ed, bowed, and sat awkwardly on the stool opposite her, gazing at her with frank appetite. Katrin's expression shifted to fear.

Maharaj's gifts were offered: another rich sari; a set of gold earrings, necklace, and nose ring; a box of sweets. A check to the Ashram had been presented to Swamiji earlier.

Brahmananda hovered with a tray. Maharaj took a brass cup filled with a liquid and offered it to Katrin. "Drink, Gauri," he said.

She refused to accept the cup.

"Drink it," Swamiji urged, with a gentle smile. "Drink."

"Drink," said Brahmananda firmly.

Katrin shook her head. The other three glanced at each other.

"Gauri Ma," said Swamiji respectfully but more forcefully, "you must accept this cup." Katrin returned his gaze with bitterness.

"Then give it to me," she said. She took the cup and drank it quickly down.

That was really the beginning of the trouble, Swamiji thought later.

☆　☆　☆

Swamiji's pacing and reviewing was interrupted by a knock at his door. This time of night – it was past midnight – no one disturbed him, but this was no ordinary night.

"*Kaun?*" he practically snapped.

"It's Narayan."

"Come, then."

Narayan entered, looking as rattled as Swamiji did. "Brahmananda Ma has come. With that American. That mage."

Swamiji stopped his pacing and squinted at Narayan. "Why? What does she want?"

"She says. . . she had a dream."

"A dream!"

"I think you should hear her, sir."

Annie was brought in. She had never been in Swamiji's most inner place, a room covered with an expensive carpet, with thickly padded cushions on low seats, and a bed, still made up. A large window was thrown open to an inky sky.

Swamiji sat down and tried to compose himself. Annie watched him force his divine smile onto a face blackened with angst. He did seem slightly unsettled by her appearance, however.

Annie had roughed up her hair, aiming for the bedhead wildness of Brent. It was about shoulder length now, longer than she had worn it in years, so it made for a pretty unusual look. She had pinched her cheeks and rubbed dirt on her eyes.

"Swamiji, I had a dream," she began without waiting for an invitation to speak. "You must tell me what it means. Not an ordinary dream. I was asleep in bed and suddenly I was sitting straight up. I heard strange sounds." He was listening intently to her, his head cocked, that was all she knew for sure. "I didn't know if I was awake or asleep. I cried out." She turned to look at Brahmananda, as if she who slept two doors down might have heard her. But Brahmananda had not been in her room all evening. "There were streaks of fire over the ashram, like laser lights or powerful fireworks. It lighted up the whole sky, it lighted up my room." Annie made broad gestures in the air, suggesting the drama in the sky in her vision. Her dirt-rimmed eyes were round and haunted. "What could this mean? I was terrified, I cried out, Who is it? Who is there?"

Annie paused theatrically.

"Then I heard the screaming of a young woman. 'Help me, save me,' she cried. Who could it be? In my dream I tried to go to her. The lights from the sky swirled around her, whether they were protecting her or destroying her, I could not tell. She screamed and screamed. I was terribly frightened."

Swamiji flinched. Annie let her story lapse for dramatic intensity, shivering at its memory.

"I thought I heard a voice call, 'I am coming, I am coming for you.' This voice was terrifying, never have I heard such a voice! And there was a crash that seemed to shake the whole ashram, even all of Rishikesh. It seemed that it started in the hills and came rushing down, rushing down with the river but greater than the riverbed, past all the places upriver and down to Rishikesh, then down to Haridwar, like a great flood. It was like a great flood that was going to destroy everything on its way. I was terrified. I have never had such a dream."

Swamiji was looking alarmed; Narayan more so. She could not see Brahmananda, who stood behind her.

"Then, in my dream, I was in the crow's nest, sipping a glass of something. I could see the sky moving overhead, and down below in the courtyard, I could see a car filling up with men, important men, who drove out and away, trying to escape the storm. But the wind and fire caught them before they got to Triveni Ghat, lifted the car and threw them against the far bank." Narayan gasped, and turned toward Swamiji. Swamiji's face had gone gray.

"And then, there was a corpse. Suddenly all went silent. I saw a corpse on a stretcher that appeared in the courtyard." Annie turned to look at Narayan. "And slowly that terrible noise began again. It grew louder and louder. The wind whirled, and picked up the stretcher with the corpse on it, and I heard a female voice saying, 'Come to me, come to me, you are mine.' It was almost singing, it became almost tender, like a mother singing to her baby. And the corpse whirled away on the wind, flying northward into the mountains.

"I watched all this from the crow's nest, until the wind subsided, and the noise and fire died, and then I awoke in my bed."

At the end of her story, Annie's voice went flat and then she said, almost as a threat: "Tell me, Swamiji, what my story means."

There was a long stunned silence in the room.

Finally Swamiji cleared his throat. "This is a most. . . unusual dream." He wasn't called on to interpret dreams very often, but he knew this was more than a dream. He looked at her suspiciously. "It is hard to say what it means." He was groping for a response.

Annie helped him out a little. Lifting an eyebrow, she asked: "Could the voice in my dream have been the Mahashakti?"

Swamiji shifted in his seat and did not want to answer. "Who knows? She comes in myriad ways. We cannot say how she will come," he said sullenly.

"But DID she come? Did she come to receive the . . . dead one?"

"How do I know! It is possible. All things are possible with Mahashakti." He waved both his hands impatiently.

"And who was the corpse in my dream?"

Swamiji leaped up angrily. "How should I know? This is just a dream! You may be nothing but a crazy woman!"

Annie stood and stretched as tall as she could, trying to be threatening. "I may be a crazy woman." She whirled to face Narayan, then back to Swamiji. "But I am a crazy woman who has seen things!" She turned around to look at Brahmananda, shrinking against a wall. "Like other crazy women in this room."

She approached Swamiji threateningly. "You have something of mine, Swami," she hissed, leaving off the '-ji.' "And I want it back!"

She whirled around to Brahmananda. "It was taken from me, and I want it back!"

There was more stunned silence in the room. "WHERE IS IT?"

Swamiji made a quick gesture. "Take it! It's nothing but an old stone."

Narayan was able to produce it almost instantly from a shelf.

"It's NOT an old stone. It is the source of my power." Annie cradled Shobha's stone, and whispered something to it.

"And now, I want Jaswanti."

"What!" Swamiji was livid. "Go! You've got your rock. Get out of here. Get out! Leave the ashram."

Narayan approached her. "You heard Swamiji. It is time for you to leave!" He was about to grab her arm, but Annie pulled it away, and shouted: "Free Jaswanti tonight. She does not want to be here. She does not belong to you. She belongs to the Mahashakti. Give her her liberty."

But Annie had got all she was going to get. Swamiji had some burly body-guards, who now appeared in the doorway. They firmly led Annie out of Swamiji's room, down the hall to the elevator, down the elevator to the front gate of the ashram, and shoved her out.

CHAPTER 24

KATRIN

After the private audience with Swamiji and his special devotees, Jaswanti was allowed to make her own way back to her room because everyone else was preoccupied with Katrin. She decided to take advantage of this little bit of unaccustomed freedom. She peeked into doors, turned down halls she hadn't seen before, checked which doors were locked and which were not. Because no one had given her bhang this evening, her mind was clear enough to master the route from her own room to the small shrine room where the tantric ceremonies took place. It was across the hall and to the left from the small audience room; this was where they took Katrin after she passed out. A turn to the right took you to the hall leading to her and Katrin's private rooms and, at the far end, the open upper verandah. Jaswanti stood for a little while watching the commotion at the entry to the small shrine; for once, no one was paying her any attention. Swamiji was directing traffic; Katrin was carried in by Narayan and Brahmananda, while Maharaj and his two assistants waited in the hall. Then Swamiji motioned to Maharaj to enter the room. After a few minutes, Swamiji and Narayan reappeared, and the door was shut. Jaswanti understood that Brahmananda was still inside, a shadowy aide to Maharaj's worship.

Still unnoticed, she made her way back to her own hall. Katrin's door was unlocked, and she went in. The brown paper wrappings from Katrin's golden sari had been neatly folded and laid by the door. A small tray with the make-up materials had been set on top of the paper to be removed. She wondered where Katrin's journal was; she found it when she pulled open the single narrow drawer of the desk.

Outside Katrin's still open window, Jaswanti saw the moon was rising over the hills. Poor Katrin! She has come from so far away and she doesn't understand our customs. She can only say a few things in our language. It is only because she is so young and beautiful that this has happened to her. Jaswanti thought this was wrong. Devi does not inhabit only young and beautiful women; Devi is in all women. It is *men* who want young and beautiful women. Old, ugly, fat men who are rich can do this to us! How can Swamiji allow this?

She sat on Katrin's bed, trying to understand her Gurudev who had honored her and Katrin and yet allowed these awful things to happen. Why not the widows? Why not Annie? This was worse than the marriage her parents had tried to arrange; at least that man had been young. And look at what Sharada's parents had done, trying to marry her to that old man in Gunapur! Why was Gurudev doing this?

Soon Jyoti Prasad would come back and she knew she would have to meet him in that room again. They would remove her clothes and she would have to sit before him naked. He would touch her. She would be dazed by bhang, but there would be no avoiding his hands, and then, the end, the hideous embrace, the smell and feel of him, the fumbling of his hardness into her. . . she remembered it and shivered, shaking her head against the memory.

She began to hear a noise coming from far off. At first she thought it was through the window, some distant cry from down at the river. She looked out and saw nothing. Then she realized the cry was coming from within the building. She crept out of Katrin's room and down the hall, past the elevator and around the corner toward the shrine room. She now heard screams, wild hysterical screaming, and then the voice of a man shouting, trying to control a situation. The door to the shrine room flew open, and Maharaj's voice could be heard shouting, "Grab her! Stop her!" His young assistant sprang in, then Swamiji and Narayan appeared from the audience chamber and ran into the shrine behind him. Jaswanti pressed against the wall, unable to move, unable not to watch.

☆　☆　☆

When Katrin regained consciousness in the shrine room, what she understood was that it was all over, the bright lights and all the strange people sitting in a strange room. That scene—lights, people, voices—had moved in and out of consciousness. There was the sound of Swamiji's voice, talking talking talking. She grasped nothing of what he was saying, but it was soothing and made her want to sleep. Then she had glided backward and slept. Now she came around and found Brahmananda undressing her; she was trying to sit upright but she so wanted to lie down and sleep. If they could just finish with her and let her sleep! It was dark, at least. There were whirling colors in the dark, a fragrant smell of flowers, of incense that her mother used to burn, the thin wafting stream of agarbatti in front of mother's little Krishna image. And she saw her mother's face, smiling, then she faded out again, feeling warm and loved.

"Katrin," whispered Brahmananda's voice, shaking her shoulder.

"Gauri Ma," came another deeper voice. She opened her eyes. There was a man, face to face with her, a huge round face, a mountain of a bare and hairy chest, a broad mouth with yellow jagged teeth. Katrin gasped, then screamed. He grabbed her by the shoulders and pressed his face to her, covering her mouth with his wet mouth. She screamed, she kept screaming, her own voice was another entity, echoing from within his mouth. Behind her, Brahmananda was ordering: "Stop! *Chup!*" She struggled, tugged away from the man's grip, tried to scramble to her feet. Now she realized her nakedness and vulnerability. She hit, she kicked, she violently bit an arm that came within reach. The man cursed and let go of her. She rose and turned on Brahmananda, beating her with her fists. She grabbed a glass vase from the table and raised it over her head; the water trickled down over her shoulder, followed by a rose. Still she screamed, waving the vase.

Maharaj backed away from the wild one, as she lunged at him with the vase. It missed him, but broke against the table. Now she had the jagged edges of glass and began to slash the air, the table, Brahmananda, and then finally herself. She slashed her left arm, over and over, still shrieking, as blood poured out of the gashes she made on her wrist. She waved this arm at Maharaj, at Brahmananda, and, when the door opened and Swamiji burst in, at her Gurudev. He looked at her with terror in his eyes as she lunged at him, streaking him with her blood.

And then, just as everyone stepped back and grasped what was happening, they saw that blood was spurting from her vein. It was one of the young assistants who thought to grab her wrist, to squeeze the vein that was pulsing blood onto the floor. She wrenched away from him and tumbled backward over the small table, knocking it and herself to the ground. They rushed to her, trying to stop the blood.

At this moment, Jaswanti, who had ventured down the hall to the open door, looked in. She took away an instant image of the scene: Maharaj, stark naked, aghast, streaked with blood; Swamiji, his white silk kurta splashed with red, help-lessly watching; Brahmananda, hand to her mouth, pressed backward against the wall; and beautiful, naked Katrin, lying on the floor, blood spurting from her arm, as Maharaj's young assistant struggled to stop the pulsing, crying, "No, no, memsahib, no."

Jaswanti backed away and fled down the hall. She ran first into Katrin's room, pulled her journal out of the drawer, stuffed it into a pillowcase, and tossed it, pil-low and all, out the open window. She then ran for the elevator, found it operable, and rode down to freedom.

Chapter 25

River's Edge

Outside the front gate of the ashram, where she had been so rudely deposited, Annie took a deep breath. She felt the silence of the great earth first on her skin, and then deeper, into her heart. There was a moon just reaching the top of the sky, nearly full, and below it, clouds with bright edges, full of rain. Beyond the steps to the ghat, the Ganges rushed over a scattering of stones and moonlight. Annie felt that this was the True Divine, these hills, this river, our planet's loyal moon, the atmosphere alive with scents and sounds, the small animals busy with their nightly work. She wanted no more myths, nor philosophies, nor practices, nor wise men leading the way, however ancient or exotic or hallowed. From here on, she wanted only the earth's simple truths.

She clutched her stone, Shobha's stone, and walked toward the river. She would have to sleep here tonight. She pulled her white sari over her head, hoping to resemble an Indian woman, and found a step along the ghat where she could lean her head on a ledge and rest. She drifted off. Something woke her after a time. There were two bare feet in front of her. She looked up an orange robe to a sadhu's weathered face. He nudged at her, waggled his head in lewd invitation. She leaped up and moved away, looking for another spot. She found a group of sleeping women, exhausted pilgrims just back from Gangotri. She joined these women, curling up beside them, feeling safety in their numbers, and went back to sleep.

☆ ☆ ☆

Jaswanti knocked anxiously at her sisters' door. Kunjlata was first to awake, to hear the knock, and open. She gasped to see Jaswanti's face. She dragged her inside, shut the door while hugging and weeping tears of joy on Jaswanti's neck. On the big bed, first Sharada, then Gitanjali awoke, looked for the sound of the noise, and then there were more suppressed shrieks, hugs, and tears.

"Tell us, tell us," they said. "What has happened? How did you escape?"

"We have to leave, we have to leave!" Jaswanti cried in desperation. "We can't stay another day. We have to go now!"

"We can't. The gates are locked." They looked at each other, four faces white with fear, trying to come up with a plan.

"At least, we have to hide Jaswanti. Come." Gitanjali led Jaswanti outside and they crept through the bushes beside their residence to where there was a water pump and a little grove of shrubs. They cocooned Jaswanti in a dark blanket and she huddled there, sleeping fitfully, until morning.

Later that night, when Brahmananda came looking for Jaswanti, Gitanjali said, "Why ask us? Ask Swamiji where she is. We'd like to see her, too."

☆ ☆ ☆

Seema could not sleep. By last check of her lighted wrist watch, it was 3:30 AM. Nic was breathing deeply by her side, always the silent sleeper. One day, maybe, he'd gurgle and snore in his sleep, or jerk awake with sleep apnea, or any of the sleep dysfunctions of old age, but that would be for Claire to deal with. When that day came, Seema could not even guess what her own situation would be. Married or dead? It was hard to imagine.

Her mind kept returning to the German girl and the scenes that probably played out afterward, in the private place where Maharaj enacted his tantric ceremony. Could the man be a serious practitioner? Or was he just enjoying a titillation with kinky trappings? Jyoti Prasad, she thought, might have been serious, more or less. Tantra done right, she had been taught, brings supernatural powers, always of interest to politicians seeking every bit of advantage. As she was brought up, in conservative Banaras although in a liberal family, she was taught to respect this tradition and its core of authentic practitioners, while understanding that most of the red-robed men she saw were free riders on society, their robes mere costumes to justify idle and decadent lives.

An hour later, her brain was still whirling. Nic had turned in his sleep, embraced her, held her tight for a while, then turned away again, never waking up. Disappointed that the embrace went nowhere, she got out of bed and plunked herself in the chair by the window, staring into the black interior of the room.

The project to get Kali away from Swamiji was proving more complicated than she had expected, now that she was up close to the situation. Before going to bed that night, she and Nic had had a long conversation about it. They both agreed that KK was integral to swamiji's ambitions; "it's the heart and soul of swami raj," Nic had said. His fame was growing by the week, drawing powerful figures to his meditation hall and audience chamber. More and more people were seeing KK. After centuries of blessed obscurity in the ugly temple in Gauhati, suddenly it was becoming a public figure. So far none of the press reports had focussed on KK, but how long until they did?

As Nic was making these points, he was walking circles in the small room, running his hands through his hair. Lal Ram had really fucked it up. Once he had accepted a deposit from Nic, he never should have let it out of his hands. What a half-assed plan, commissioning a look-alike sculpture! How long was that going to take? How was the switch going to happen? He was going to call him in the morning and tell him to get himself to Rishikesh and solve this problem.

Seema continued to obsess over the German girl. "Just think what it must have been like for her!"

"What do you mean?"

"Obvious what was going on! I mean when she was taken into that room with Maharaj. That awful old man!"

Nic was trying to imagine the scene, but somehow in his imagination it was always him in the role of tantric practitioner, a tantalizing thought. Katrin looked like a girl he had once thought he was in love with. Lots of blonde hair, pale blue eyes, pure white skin, long, long legs. He heard how angry Seema was, but couldn't get there.

"She came here looking for it, remember."

"Looking for what?!"

He shrugged.

By the time her watch showed 5:30, Seema put on clothes and left the room, leaving Nic asleep behind her. As soon as she was outdoors, she felt invigorated by the dawn air. The sky was gray but clean-smelling, promising more scrubbing of the filth that clung to the broad leaves of peepul trees along the path toward the river. Ganga washes away all sins, and Seema wanted to bathe.

Along the concrete ghats at river's edge, life was already stirring. Upriver, there were huts built right out on the gravel shoulders of the river, where destitute young families lived; mothers were lighting tiny fires while sleepy children squatted to defecate nearby. Closer, sadhus waded into the river to wash, scooping up water over their heads and sipping it from cupped hands. Seema waded in, too, splashing her arms and face, but had better sense than to drink it.

The little group of saffron-robed women that Annie had joined in the middle of the night was now stirring, and Annie woke up, relieved to learn it was morning and the awful night was over. After using Shobha's stone for a pillow and only the concrete ghat for a mattress, her head was swollen and her neck felt stuffed with straw. She stumbled to her feet. As she did so, the horrors of the night came flooding back. But – breathing deeply – there was that river, ceaselessly rushing out of the mountains, there were those hills, and the ever-changing heavens. This was real; could last night have been illusion?

"You were there last night, weren't you?" said a voice. Annie turned to see Seema standing on a lower step of the ghat.

"Yes." Annie looked at her, puzzled, trying to remember. "You were at the audience."

"I thought you were living at the ashram," Seema said, taking in Annie's disarray.

"They threw me out."

"What! Why?"

Annie gave Seema a long look, trying to judge her character. Should she trust her? "Do you know what happened last night? Afterward?" She needed someone to talk to.

"Why don't you tell me. My name is Seema."

And so they sat on the steps by the river, as Annie told Seema everything she saw and did the night before. Seema gasped at certain points, uttering low 'oh my god's' from time to time.

"The girl is certainly dead," she said, when Annie described the body being taken away on the stretcher. "But how did she die?"

"Maybe from an overdose? I don't know. How will it affect Swamiji? He can't really cover this up. Though he is trying."

"No. It won't be possible." Seema thought about it. "Someone needs to call the police." She didn't want it to be her, however. She wanted to stay far away from any public investigation, and Nic absolutely had to stay out of sight. Probably he should get out of town.

"I'm not going to the police station; I'm a foreigner." Annie tried to think. "I know how to contact the police. I have a friend who is a doctor."

"Yes, let the doctor call. We are just leaving today, and we didn't see anything more than others at the audience, so we are hardly witnesses. What is your name, by the way?"

"Sorry I don't have a card. I'm Annie Gilbert."

☆　☆　☆

Dr. Gupta was having her morning tea before meeting her first patients, enjoying a cool morning on a day that promised more rainy relief from the heat. Every day, she reflected, was a day of trying to help suffering people, usually women and children because she specialized in that. There was more suffering than anyone could do anything about, day after day she barely dented the troubles of the good people who appeared at her clinic. Would she ever be able to stop? She thought of Annie, the American with the time and freedom to be traveling in India. What a joy that would be! She doubted it was for her, however; it was her karma to work on peoples' suffering bodies until her own gave out on her.

She hadn't seen Annie or had an update on the goings on at Bhav Dham Ashram in a while. She wondered what was going on with the German girl they were claiming was Gauri. What a racket that swami had going! Something should be done about him. She detested these religious entrepreneurs, who could be doing something useful about all the suffering in the world and instead were adding to it.

Over the course of the next hour, five refugees from the ashram showed up at her door. First came Annie, haggard after a night sleeping on hard earth with a triangular stone for a pillow. Dr. Gupta gave her a long, appraising look. "You should wash your face, Annie. There is mud all over it." Then she burst out laughing.

Annie rubbed her eyes, shook her head, and said, "If you only knew!" Patting down her hair into something less alarming than its present disarray, she added, "I was sort of in costume."

"Sit down and tell me the latest news from the ashram. Somehow I doubt it's going to be a nice story." She called for another pot of tea.

Annie recounted the scene in the rear courtyard of the ashram and her dramatic performance for Swamiji. "They must know that I saw everything. My performance only frightened them for a moment and they wanted to get me out of their sight. But I'm pretty sure they'll think more clearly this morning and decide that I am a dangerous witness."

"You took a tremendous chance, Annie. You should have come straight here, and we could have called the police last night. Which is what I am going to do right now." She reached for her telephone, putting her glasses back on so she could look up the number on a sheet of paper taped to her desk.

"Where would they have taken Katrin's body?"

"To the cremation ground. It's burned by now, you can be sure of that."

By the time two officers arrived from the Lakshman Jhula station, and Dr. Gupta went through her still empty clinic to let them in, Jaswanti and her sisters were sitting quietly outside with the assembling mothers and children. "Wh-, what's this!" She exclaimed, doing a double take. "Is it you, Jaswanti? Come." She hurried them into her office along with the police officers.

Sub-Inspector Mishra took control, amid the commotion of so many excited women. He was a large man who wore a stern expression as official as his shirt and badge, essential aspects of his authority.

"Now, Dr. Gupta, what is it?" he began, directing his attention to the doctor. Annie was sitting off to the side of the big desk, and the four sisters were aligned along a bench facing it.

"We have reason to believe there may have been a drug overdose and death last night at Bhav Dham Ashram. Perhaps it has already been reported to you by the officials there?"

"Nothing has been reported to us," he said gruffly, as if that fact alone made him doubt what he was about to hear.

"Perhaps Annie should tell you what she saw last evening."

Annie turned to him and began describing the scene in the audience hall, when Katrin had looked heavily drugged and finally passed out, and then the scene later on, as Maharaj fled and the body was brought out.

"Madam, where are you from?" he asked sternly, as if her foreignness were a further suspicious fact.

"America. Sir."

"And the girl, where did you say she was from?"

"Germany."

He was silent while processing this information. "And where are these drugs coming from?" The implication was all too clear.

"Officer," said Dr. Gupta, matching stern with stern. "This is not about foreigners and drugs. This is our own home-grown variety, bhang and ganja used by our swamis and sadhus. Shaktinandan has been using bhang in old-fashioned tantric pujas. It's just that in this one case, a very young foreign girl got swept up in it and suffered a dreadful consequence."

He processed this information, then took out his cell phone and called the station. In curt tones oft repeated, he ordered someone to the cremation ground to stop until further notice any burnings that may be in process.

No one had yet thought to ask what Jaswanti might have to say, and she herself was too modest to speak out, unasked, and she was still in shock over the scene she had witnessed the night before. She was clutching a small book inside a pillowcase. After she and her sisters rather easily walked out of the front gate once it was unlocked in the morning, they had gone around to the side of the ashram and searched in the bushes until they found the bundle she had thrown out the window the night before. She was thinking of the book as a precious reminder of her friend, not as evidence in a police investigation.

"Okay, I am going now. Give me your names, please." He wrote down everyone's names. "Do not leave Rishikesh," he ordered Annie and the sisters. "We may need to talk to you later."

Chapter 26

All Quiet

"I understand, I understand," Nic was saying with precarious courtesy into his cell phone. "I am just trying to say that it has to move faster. This deal is going to fall apart if we can't make some. . . adjustments. And quickly." He was talking to Lal Ram, who didn't sound entirely awake on the other end of the line. He was probably still having his tea in bed in Banaras.

Seema came quietly into the room and sat down to listen to the rest of the conversation. Nic waved a kiss to her.

"What I am trying to explain, my friend, is that this 'piece' is becoming too prominent. Too many people are seeing it. It's the center of a, shall we say, a religious movement. Some very important people are now involved."

Seema made a gesture with her hands that attempted to convey 'big news.'

'What?' Nic said with his lips.

"I think you should come here and see what's going on. I'd really feel better if you were on the scene. Otherwise, I fear we're going to have to cut our losses."

Seema could hear the voice on the other end protesting. "Okay, that's good news. Yes. As soon as possible. All right. Until then, yes, goodbye." He poked the red 'off' bar on his iPhone.

"He's coming," he said. "Okay, what's your news?"

"The German girl is dead. Apparently she died of the overdose we saw, and her body was slipped out the back door in the middle of the night. Right after Maharaj took off on the run."

"Omigod." Nic slumped down onto the bed. "The police are going to be all over this."

"And after that, the press."

They chewed on this in silence for a few minutes.

"You have to get out of town. I should stay to keep an eye on things. I won't attract any attention."

Nic ruminated on this. He was a high profile art dealer, a lot of people knew who he was. He had been to Swamiji's private audiences two nights in a row. He couldn't risk being associated with any investigations; people would wonder what he was doing here. Any stories he made up about becoming interested in Hinduism might also make news. Some people might wonder why the scion of a large international art house would be taking up with a swami in Rishikesh. They would look around the premises, wondering what he saw when he looked around. There was practically a spotlight, a neon sign, pointing to KK.

"Okay, I'm on my way."

"I'll go arrange for a car." Seema left the room, while Nic began throwing his things back into his suitcase.

☆ ☆ ☆

Annie became a denizen of the little western world around the coffee shops and hang-outs on the western hillside above Rishkesh. She gave up *jap* and satsang, and replaced her white novice's sari with jeans and some colorful kurtas bought in the market. She managed to retrieve her laptop from Tyagi Ma and her suitcase and books from her former room at the ashram. She enjoyed drinking coffee on the terrace while puzzling over the computer textbooks under the sheltering bougainvillea and mimosa trees, with no one monitoring her conduct.

For the next few days, people in the know crept around their usual haunts waiting for news to break. Annie didn't know what was going on in the ashram, except that when Tyagi Ma and another of the widows met her at the back gate with her laptop and suitcase and books, Tyagi Ma whispered, "Things are very tense." Beyond that, she could not say in front of the other widow. "Have the police come?" Annie persisted, but Tyagi Ma replied, "I don't know anything about it," and scooted away.

There seemed to be more people on hand at Lonnie's than usual, and Annie knew many of them. There was Seema, the beautiful young woman from that last audience, whom she had finally met at riverside, who like her was a refugee from the ashram. There was Brent, still around, strumming his guitar. Annie didn't know whether he still went to satsang. Several other couples from the last audience seemed to have taken up residence at Lonnie's.

Lonnie herself was the local news anchor, acquiring and passing information and analysis to the little republic in her courtyard. Yes, she had learned, the police had gone to talk to Swamiji. They also interviewed Narayan and Brahmananda and several of the widows. It had been too late to recover Katrin's body; it was already burned. No mention of Jaswanti.

There was finally a small notice in the Garhwal Post regarding the accidental death of a foreigner in an unnamed Rishikesh ashram. The German embassy was informing the family of an unnamed German national who died under unknown circumstances last week.

Everyone at Lonnie's gathered around the paper as Lonnie read the brief notice.

"Can you believe that!" Annie exclaimed.

"Totally brushed under the table, the bastards," Lonnie said. Seema, also standing by, registered relief, then guilt.

✧ ✧ ✧

Lal Ram arrived two days after Nic's rushed departure. Seema met him at a cheap family hotel down in the town, far from the ashrams on the northern edge. They walked out toward Triveni Ghat to talk. As he approached the river, he stopped, brought his hands together in reverent namaskar to Gangaji. The goddess/river looked so different, so young, here in the mountains. At Banaras she was a voluptuous, fat, mid-life goddess; here she was vivacious, slim, quick-moving. He loved all her moods, all her forms.

"Where is Grayson Sahib?" he asked, first thing.

"He could not stay. It was too risky. He's gone back to Delhi. In fact, he's had to leave for London. Some important business." She waved her wrist dismissively. Nic is gone; deal with me.

"Ah," he said, greatly disappointed.

"But I am here, representing him," she added quickly. "We have a problem, as you know."

"Yes, yes, I'll certainly do everything I can," but he didn't sound as certain as his words.

"You must talk to Swamiji. He's your gurudev. You must get him to give up the murti. Even if the replacement isn't yet ready."

Lal Ram tried to think through how this conversation would go. His gurudev was compassionate, of that he had no doubt. Yet he could sometimes be moody, and maybe a little snappish. This was a conversation he did not want to have; but business was business, and his family had to eat. Maybe he could make that point, too. He was not ready to leave the world to take sanyas, as some day he would do. He was still a *grihast*, he had family responsibilities. What could he do? He would spread his hands, showing he had tried to think of anything else, but there was no other solution. Still, he wasn't optimistic.

"If you can get him to give it up, it should be shipped directly to your godown in Delhi. From there, Nic can see it gets to the UK." This was actually part of Seema's job, as there could be no Grayson fingerprints on the transfer, but she didn't need to tell him that.

"Under no circumstances should you mention Nic to your gurudev. I hope that is perfectly clear."

"Yes, perfectly."

✼   ✼   ✼

Lal Ram had been dismayed to learn that Nic and Seema had discovered who his gurudev was – he had no idea how – and had come to Rishikesh to meet him. He thought it was foolhardy in the extreme, this meddling in affairs the Englishman really couldn't understand. Seema should have been a wiser head. Of course it was obvious she was under his spell, or he under hers. This all would have worked out if they had just let him do things his way.

He had called the ashram to set up a time for a private meeting with Swamiji. Lal Ram was the kind of devotee that got this kind of treatment; he made large donations and came from an important merchant family in Banaras. He arrived right on time, walked through the main gate where the vikram deposited him, and was met by Narayan. Narayan was always courteous, generally deferential, and never warm. He led him into Swamiji's private audience room.

Swamiji had on his usual half-lidded serenity, as he sat on his seat against the wall, the only real chair in the room. Lal Ram touched his feet in reverence, then settled himself on the carpet. Narayan moved to the back of the room and sat against the wall as if napping. Lal Ram waited for Swamiji to speak first. Swamiji extended the silence. The room arrangement, the foot-touching, the silence all reinforced the hierarchy of their relationship. Finally he spoke.

"How is it with your family?"

"All are well, thank you."

"And you are well?"

"For the most part, yes, swamiji."

"You have come all this way. We don't generally see you here."

"Yes, swamiji. I've come on a delicate matter. I could not wait until your next trip to Banaras."

"We are most grateful to you," said Swamiji, not letting Lal Ram get on to his delicate matter. "We wish to say that your gift to the ashram has produced great fruits." For 'gift' he used the word *dan*, suggesting a great religious gift, such as from a king to a temple. Lal Ram's heart sank. One cannot take back *dan*. That wasn't the language they had used back in Banaras, when Swamiji had been invited to Durga Puja and asked about the beautiful Kali. Lal Ram had explained that it was in transit, so to speak, from a poor Brahmin family in Assam to a purchaser in South India. The family had just 'borrowed' it a little bit for Durga Puja. He had left it vague. Swamiji had tried to make a better offer, asking how much the South Indian buyer was paying, then offering twice that. But Lal Ram had regretfully said he had already accepted a payment; he couldn't break the contract. Swamiji had mulled this over for a few hours, then made a proposal: suppose he took it on loan for just a few months? It shouldn't, after all, be crated up in wood and straw in a warehouse; he would care for Kaliji, and then they could consider a replacement. His ashram was Vishnuite, after all; there had never been a major Kali influence. But who could have imagined the way in which Kali had flowed through this murti in the last few months? It was inconceivable to crate her back up, as if she were nothing but a lump of stone.

All this was implied and understood, as Lal Ram processed the simple word *dan*. He was defeated.

"Now what is your delicate matter, Lal Ram?" inquired Swamiji sweetly.

Lal Ram fumbled for a delicate matter important enough to justify a trip half way across India. He started with a story about his business, weaker these days, perhaps should open another outlet, or else close one, assigning his various younger brothers to this or that function, ending on a note of confusion. "As you can see, Swamiji," he said, spreading his hands helplessly, "I am all in turmoil these days. I need your guidance."

Swamiji nodded wisely, and delivered a little sermonette about karma and maya and desire and the need to start withdrawing from life's grip. Lal Ram nodded meekly, submitting to his gurudev, and later on he did feel a little bit better.

☆ ☆ ☆

The conversation with Seema later that day did not go well. He reached her by cell phone as she was sitting in the courtyard at Lonnie's. Seema refused to accept that the situation was past saving. Lal Ram apologized abjectly, he was totally over a barrel, there was nothing that could be done at this point. He would refund Grayson Sahib's deposit in full.

Seema was livid. "This cannot happen this way!" she hissed into her cell phone. There were people at nearby tables, pretending not to hear. "What happened?"

"He won't give it up. What can I do? He has possession of it," the voice on the other end whined. "I can't call in the police on this matter, can I? It's not a matter for the police." Lal Ram's excuse contained a threat.

"No, of course not." She thought fast, seeking a solution where there was none. "This is a very bad development, bhaisahib!" She steamed; he apologized a few more times. "Okay. All right. It's over. See that a refund check arrives by next Monday."

Annie was at another table, talking intently to Brent. He had become surprisingly friendly with her, full of questions about life in the ashram. He learned that Seema had been in the private audience THAT night, and he tried pull her into conversation, too. As Seema slapped her cell phone onto the table in anger, Brent called to her, "Don't hurt your phone!"

Seema put on a laugh. "It's the one on the other end I'd like to hurt!" She continued to steam, but with a pleasanter look on her face, while half-listening to the conversation at the next table. It almost sounded like Brent was interviewing Annie.

Brent had asked how she happened to be drawn into the inner circle at the ashram, and Annie began describing the incident with the black stone, how it had disappeared from her suitcase, and the same night she was summoned to his private audience, how he had just appropriated it from her. Seema was paying close attention now.

"Why would he care about this black stone when he's got that fabulous Kali?" Brent wondered.

"His story is, he doesn't 'get' them; they come to him. It's a good line. They show up, or they fly to him, from someplace like Kamakhya, in the case of the big one in the meditation hall," Annie said. "I don't know how he got that one, but the little one, he stole right out of my suitcase!" They laughed at the audacity of the swami, who seemed to be as untouchable as he was outrageous.

"I was there the night blood appeared on the face of Kali," Annie said. "It seemed so obvious that someone must have flung a baggie of blood at it while the lights were out."

"No," Brent said, "that's not how it happened. Have you looked close? There's a hole in the middle of her forehead. And it goes through to the back of her head.

All they have to do is have someone in the back with a rubber pump, pumping it through!" This evoked gales of laughter.

"How can people buy this?" Annie wondered.

"Actually, Annie," he said, lowering his voice, "I've heard something about this image. When I was in Delhi, I heard a story about a valuable antiquity that was being smuggled out of the country. One detail astonished me: it had a hole and a tube that would allow blood or ash to be blown through from the back. I was coming here for my research on the Maharishi, but just before leaving Delhi there was a story in the papers about this politician and this tantric swami, so I decided to look in on him, too, while I was here. Then I saw that Kali – and saw the hole in her head! It has to be the same one I heard about."

Annie was puzzled. "But, it's not being smuggled. It's right here."

"I don't know. I haven't figured that out yet. How many can there be? 'Gorgeous Kali with hole in head.' I don't think Shaktinandan is going to let it out of his hands."

Seema, listening to this conversation, began to calm down. She had to let KK go. She turned her mind to alternatives, and slowly her heart stopped its racing. She sat there for another hour, half-listening to Brent pump Annie for information about Swamiji, while she planned her next move. 'Sorry, Nic,' she thought. The next morning, she took a car to Dehra Dun, where she caught a flight back to Gauhati.

✵ ✵ ✵

Jaswanti sheltered with her sisters in a tiny spare room in Dr. Gupta's private apartment, where each night they unrolled a mat almost the same size as the room, and slept side by side, their heads near a single open window. Some nights they carried the mattress to the roof where there was more air under the open sky.

Jaswanti cried much of every day, unable to shake the horrible scene. There was always at least one sister sitting quietly with an arm around her, and Jaswanti would lean on her shoulder, soaking her sari with tears, until she fell asleep from emotional exhaustion. Dr. Gupta watched over these scenes, with one eye on the calendar. She would give Jaswanti a week to grieve, then she intended to put her to work. Service would heal the young woman's wounds, she was certain, better than any other remedy.

No one from the police ever asked to interview her. Dr. Gupta talked to Officer Mishra from time to time, and learned that they had accepted the ashram's account of the German girl's death. She had come to the ashram as a highly motivated seeker, and after severe tapasya over several months – perhaps more than she, a foreigner, was really ready for – she had come to a high spiritual plane, achieving bhav readily, in long-lasting episodes. In this, she was assisted by drafts of bhang, an ancient tradition in India, particularly among tantrics. While there were severe laws against the drug trade in India, small amounts of ganja, hashish, and bhang were generally overlooked, and usage was widespread during great holidays like Holi. In this case, the death appeared to be some kind of psychotic break leading to suicide. Swami Shaktinandan was deeply grieved over it, and in fact the whole ashram was in mourning. He seemed to be blaming himself for not restraining the religious fervor of some of his followers, and Officer Mishra went so far as to urge him not to be too harsh with himself. Many of these foreigners were naive and foolish in their embrace of customs they did not understand.

As Dr. Gupta came to understand the police view, she thought any interview with Jaswanti would not change the police perception of events, and would be exceedingly hard on the girl. She was a victim, too, and Dr. Gupta's concern was for her healing, not for law enforcement that, in any case, was not going to put a stop to the swami.

A week after the arrival of the sisters, Dr. Gupta put them to work. She taught Gitanjali how to operate the little machine that pumped up the black cuff of the aneroid manometer and listen through the stethoscope to record blood pressure. After a few days of checking her readings, she concluded that Gitanjali could be relied upon to get it right. Jaswanti was usually given tasks with babies, washing their faces, noses, and ears with soapy water, bouncing them gently while their mothers were seen by Dr. Gupta, soothing them after their injections. All the girls assisted with sterilizing equipment, cleaning the anteroom and the two small examination rooms, and stocking supplies. Dr. Gupta gave them frequent little lessons in sanitation, infectious agents, routes of infection transmission, and safe methods of disposal of hospital waste.

In the evenings, they often ate with Dr. Gupta on the roof, sitting cross-legged on the ground, eating from brass thalis in front of them, laughing at events of the day. They still did jap and sang bhajans in mornings and evenings, but the needs of the clinic came to fill their days – and their minds and hearts – with useful work.

One night on the roof, as they were finishing a meal of yogurt and chapattis that they had also cooked, Sharada said, "We were going to become traveling sadvi, weren't we?"

There was a little pause while everyone thought back to that idea, when they had been so desperate to rescue Jaswanti and escape.

"It's romantic," Kunjlata observed, "getting on trains, riding from temple to temple to temple, sleeping under trees."

"Annie slept under a tree with some old sadvi. . . that night," said Sharada. "She was very sore the next day!"

"Imagine that, night after night!"

"And you have to beg for food."

"I could do it," Sharada insisted, "If that were the only way. But maybe this is a more useful path."

"We are doing good here," Jaswanti said, "and Dr. Gupta is the best gurudev we could have."

CHAPTER 27

SHOBA

A nnie was not recovering from the abnormal elation she felt at her new-found freedom. She did not come down from this high. Every morning she woke thrilled to a new day of perfect independence. The weeks she had spent in the ashram had been weeks of external control, the oppression of strong moralistic rules intended to produce, oddly enough, liberation. Now that she was out of that environment, she felt liberated! No more satsang! No more jap! It was the second stage of her personal liberation, following the one that began the moment she backed out of the flip-house on Junot Street and out of Ted's life. If depression and alienation were ahead for her, it was hard to imagine how it would come.

Still, she had to plan her future. Where would she go when she left Rishikesh? She wasn't sure. It would not be back to Ted. Would it be back to the States? Even of that she wasn't sure. Maybe she owed Ted slightly more explanation than he had got from her so far, but she didn't ever want to have to sit down face to face with him while explaining herself. The time for that was long past. It could be an exchange of emails . . . which would quickly turn into flame wars. Maybe just a long letter via snail mail. She was in no rush.

Every few days she walked down to the clinic to talk to Gitanjali, Jaswanti, and the others. They were usually busy with tasks around the clinic, their minds now focused on helping the sick mothers and children who endlessly awaited Dr. Gupta's ministrations. Gitanjali confided to Annie that Dr. Gupta had talked about sending her for nurse's training in Dehra Dun.

"Would you like that?"

"Oh, yes, Annie!"

For just a moment Annie wished she were young again and could start a new career, too. What would it be? Not nursing. Doing exactly what she was doing now was the career she wanted; but what name to give it?

One afternoon as Annie ambled onto the coffee terrace, she saw there were two new persons ordering from the menu. She knew immediately who they must be. One was a European woman, the other a younger Indian woman. She sat down at a table from which she could watch them unobtrusively. The Indian woman was in her late twenties, and dressed in the white of a young ashram novice. She had unusually thick black hair that frizzed outside its long braid, creating a shadowy halo around her head. She had soft black eyes, thick perfect brows, and pale skin.

Annie left her books on the table to return to her room, and was back by the time the two women finished ordering.

"Are you, by any chance, Shobha?" she asked.

Shobha looked up at her in surprise. "Yes."

Annie set the stone, now wrapped in a new piece of red silk from the market, in front of Shobha. "This is yours, I believe." Shobha looked at the stone, then back at Annie.

"You must be Karen's friend," Erika said.

Shobha and Erika had just returned from the Char Dham Yatra, the long journey to all the major pilgrimage sites north of Rishikesh. They had traveled by private car, by bus, and on foot, in the way of modern pilgrims, for six weeks. First they had gone to Yamunotri, the extreme northwest of the sacred places, then backtracked to Uttarkashi and then up to Gangotri. From Gangotri they made an extra trek, solely on foot, to Gaumukh, the very spot where Ganga flows out of the Gangotri glacier. "This is its very source, Annie, the 'cow's mouth.'" Then they had to retrace their route to the access point for the next narrow valley to Kedernath, and then again to the next eastward valley, the Valley of Flowers, to Badrinath. "And we just got back last night."

Shobha spoke in a soft voice, in perfect English, evidence of her excellent education. Annie was trying to remember all the things Karen had told her about Shobha. A rich family from Dehra Dun who didn't want her going into an ashram. Domineering father, supportive mother. Meanwhile, Shobha was tenderly fondling the stone under its silk wrapping.

"Thank you so much for bringing this, Annie. It is so precious to me. And to my family."

"But why did you give it to Karen last summer?"

"Annie, things were going on at the ashram that. . . worried me."

"Have you heard what's been going on while you were gone?"

"No. Tell me."

"Good heavens! Why don't we start with last summer? Then I'll catch you up."

"Well, okay. You see, Swamiji began talking about Devi. You know about Devi, Annie?"

Annie nodded. "I've gotten familiar with some things."

"He had a dream, or maybe several of them. Devi was coming to him, he said. She wanted more devotion from people around here. There was plenty of yoga, of meditation, of Vishnu and Krishna, and of course Shiva. And Ganga. But who was worshipping her? Was not her father Himalaya himself? And yet for real devotees, Devi had to look east, to eastern India. So she was calling him."

Erika said, "I shouldn't be cynical, but there was a niche here."

"Of course there are some Devi temples in Rishikesh, but Swamiji wanted something more for Bhav Dham Ashram. He began talking about foreigners and rich Indians who were interested in tantra." Shobha shook her head. "This was my Gurudev, I loved him more than anything. I would do anything for him. But I began to wonder why he was so ambitious. It did not seem. . . godly.

"When I came to the ashram, he knew that I brought with me our family *svayambhu*, our self-revealed Mother that has been in our family for many generations. It was found on land my ancestors owned. It has many stories that Swamiji asked me to tell him. He began to have dreams about it.

"Then he began to call me the incarnation of that Mother. I asked him what this meant, but I could never take his meaning. I think that actually he was trying to figure out himself where to go with this idea. One time he gave me a drink, a very bad drink that some old sadhus take, and it had a terrible effect on me. My mind became clouded, and I felt I was floating, and I had visions, not holy ones but chaotic ones that had no sense or significance. He led me into a small room in this state and began to worship me. He put flowers on my head and chanted and sprinkled holy water from a *lota*. This much, at least, I could understand and remember later on.

"Afterward, when I came to my senses again, I thought that this was not a good thing. I came to the ashram to worship, not to be worshipped. I wanted to follow my Gurudev, not to be followed by him. I thought the *svyambhu* of our family was going to be misused. And so I gave it to Karen, my good friend, who was going back to the United States. I knew she would keep it safe for me, and later I could always get it back."

"And then you sent a message that you wanted it back?"

"Yes. In May my father died. Of course this was a great tragedy for my mother. For all of us." Shobha paused respectfully. "But, my father was a very strong man and did not approve of so much religion. For instance, he never wanted me to come into this life. He tried to forbid me, but I kept running away to Gurudev, and finally he had to agree to it, even after he had a marriage arranged for me. But after my father died, my mother came into her own life. My family has property and houses in many places. My mother asked me if there was anything that I wanted? I have no brother to take over all these things, because my one brother died in a motorcycle accident five years ago. So now all this wealth belongs to my mother and my sister and myself. I said yes. There is one property that I want. That is the house at Devprayag. Have you been there, Annie? This is a beautiful town seventy kilometers from here, at a place where the Alakananda and Bhagirathi come together to form the Ganga. Our house is on the bank right at the confluence. It needs some repairs, but I am going to establish an ashram there, just for women. I have come back to meet with architects to begin this project."

"Shobha, this is a marvellous idea!"

Shobha smiled one of her rare smiles. "Do you think so? And of course I have to inform Swamiji. He will not like this."

"I don't think that's going to be a problem, under the circumstances."

"Well, thank you for return our *svayambhu mata*. She will be the main deity in the shrine. Along with Lord Krishna, of course."

After relinquishing the black stone, Shobha's Stone, Annie continued to feel a mysterious and permanent attachment to it, as if, after all, it had powers to call and influence people. It was a large and inconveniently weighty thing to have carried around for all these weeks, and she felt lighter without it, as well as relieved, but it had altered her in real ways. It had brought her to India; to Rishikesh; to the ashram; to Swamiji. For its sake, she had spun fantasies and dreams – her mage self – and offered them to others as definitions of her. She had sometimes thought how it wanted to be reunited with Shobha, with Annie its agent. Shobha's Stone, the *svayambhu mata*, had a kind of life itself, and Annie had been drawn into its orbit. It would now go to Devprayag, to be enshrined in Shobha's new ashram at the convergence of the Alakananda and Bhagirathi, and go on uniting people in love and community. Annie had been part of its biography, and that was a surprising thing.

✳ ✳ ✳

She stayed at Lonnie's for another month, while deciding where to go once she left Rishikesh. She had good friends here – though some, like Brent and Seema, were gone – all people she would never have known if she had not left home. She had time to hike all over the area, both sides of the river, including far north above Lakshman Jhula. One day she slipped past the signs and gates marking off the Maharishi's former ashram, and explored the cluster of beehive rooms where the Beatles had stayed. There were hanging wasps' nests and invasions of grasses and forest shrubs, plus trash and graffiti, and this proof of the impermanence of life and the endurance of the earth filled her with joy.

Lonnie continued to be the news anchor for the Europeans on the hill, but since Annie no longer had insider knowledge of affairs at the ashram, it was only by second hand that she learned what happened about six weeks after THAT NIGHT when everything changed.

Unexpected visitors arrived at the front gate of the ashram. They were not dressed in street clothes; nor were they dressed in the white robes of an ashram novice, the usual uniform of followers or seekers. They wore dhotis in the old-fashioned *satvik* way of rural Brahmins, the edge of the cloth pulled between their legs and tucked into the back, looking like long bloomers. They were shirtless, which allowed their sacred threads to be seen across their broad chests.

Narayan was sent for, and he duly met them with puzzled courtesy. They were haughty as only Brahmins can be to religious professionals of lower caste; they knew Narayan was a Kayastha. They demanded to be taken to Shaktinandan. They did not say 'swamiji.' Narayan delayed by installing them in a small waiting room just off Swamiji's private audience room. He left them there for forty-five minutes and would have left them longer, except that two cars of policemen pulled up at the same gate, also demanding to see Shaktinandan.

By this time, most of the ashram residents were alerted to something going on, and a crowd of white and saffron robed onlookers was growing in the central courtyard.

Swamiji appeared at the door to his residence.

"Central Bureau of Investigation," said the officer in charge, a large man with wide shoulders and a trim mustache. Onlookers turned to each other with open mouths. Swamiji looked startled. "I am Officer Shrivastava. You are in possession of an unregistered antiquity, illegally removed from its original place."

Swamiji's eyebrows flew up in astonishment. "No, sir," he said, shaking his head.

"A black marble Kali murti belonging to Kamakhya Temple in Assam State is not in your possession?" His voice was stern and frightening.

"Ah, maybe. . . ah, there could be some misunderstanding." Swamiji, flushed and disoriented, seemed tongue-tied and rooted in place.

"Please take us to your murti."

At this point, the three Brahmins, who had found their way out of the building, scowling, joined the little group of officers in the middle of the big group of onlookers. "This Kali was taken from our place," one of them said. "It belongs to Kamakhya."

Swamiji without further delay led the group to his meditation hall, where they stopped in the doorway to gaze at graceful Kali, standing high over the other deities behind the dais. They caught their breath in admiration. The Brahmins elaborately namaskared their lost – and found – goddess. After a few moments of this, there were more self-important and disapproving frowns all around.

"How did this image come into your possession?" demanded Srivastava.

Swamiji had had time, in the walk across the courtyard, to think of the answer to this.

"It is merely on loan," he said. "One of my devoted followers loaned it to me after Durga Puja. I did not ask if there was any problem with it. I am only learning now that there may be a problem. And still I do not know what it might be. Perhaps the officer might explain to me?"

"It is an antiquity over one hundred years old. . . ,"

"It is over five hundred years old!" asserted one of the Brahmins.

". . . and thus cannot be moved and must be registered in its original place and by anyone who has it in possession."

"So then it is illegal for it not to be in Kamakhya, is this what I am to understand?"

"Yes," said Officer Srivastava.

"Yes!" said several of the Brahmins in unison.

"Well, then, it must go back!" said Swamiji smoothly. "I had no idea. Would I wish to be on bad terms with Kamakhya?" he asked, spreading his hands.

☆ ☆ ☆

Things settled down, after that, not too different from how things had always been at Bhav Dham Ashram. The events of that summer had an impact on a number of people who later on went their ways.

Nic stayed busy in London for two years before he thought it wise to visit India again. Seema went back to work at the museum, feeling chastened after her brief infatuation with Nic and under his influence conspiring to sell off India's patrimony to foreigners.

The following June she published an academic paper entitled: "The Social Life of Kamakhya Kali," in which she traced the history of this particular image from its production in Orissa workshops, to emplacement at the famous Kamakhya Temple in Gauhati, Assam. There was a section on the period of incursions of Muslim conquerors, with their religious imperative to destroy false images. She dealt at length with the uncertain evidence about which commanders came to Assam, and when, and she described efforts taken by Brahmins across North India to protect their deities and other sacred items, sometimes burying them, sometimes coating them with plaster and tucking them away into insignificant locations.

Another lengthy section dealt with the Brahmin lineages involved in the dispute over ownership once it was safe to bring Kamakhya Kali back out from her hiding place. There was a kinship diagram showing the generations of descent to the present, and the several branches that continued to dispute ownership.

A somewhat tongue-in-cheek section dealt with the hole in Kali's head, allowing for some trickery on the part of Brahmins. This was not actually so unusual, as there were other documented images, such as one with movable arms, that enabled temple officials to treat the pious to little miracles, but most Brahmins were disapproving of such stunts and Kamakhya Kali had probably not been used in this way for a very long time – until recently.

Then came a section making the argument that the uncontrolled pilfering of the eighteenth and nineteenth centuries was at least as devastating as anything the Muslims did centuries earlier, with carvings hacked away from walls, frescoes peeled off the walls of caves, and images stolen out of villages by dead of night. To this day, the black market in Indian antiquities is only nominally controlled, although – final section – the most recent moment in Kamakhya Kali's astonishing history did have a satisfying conclusion. Here she could describe Kali's travels across North India and her brief, aborted visitation at Bhav Dham Ashram in Rishikesh. This section was handled delicately, not to lead attention to any London art trader or his Indian agents. Finally, Kamakhya Kali is back at home, to the place where her eyes were first painted open in the fifteenth century, her home temple in Assam. The paper was a real tour de force.

It took two years for Brent to get his book out. *Swami: From Maharishi to Osho* was deftly written, with a great deal of first-person detail, making unusually interesting reading for an academic book. In the introduction he described the way he sauntered around India with his guitar, hanging out in cafes and bars and ashrams, getting to know local people and hearing local stories, a good many of which would be recounted in subsequent chapters. While in Delhi seeking out some Osho followers (who had first encountered him as Rajneesh in Oregon) he read in the paper about a rising tantric group in Rishikesh, and so he made his way north just at the time when this group was imploding. Annie had an unnamed cameo appearance as "an excellent insider source" at the ashram, who provided background detail on the workings of the ashram and an introduction to Jaswanti, renamed Sita for the book. His last chapter presented the dark side of the fascination with tantra and the dangers of unquestioning allegiance to swamis. Here, for the first time, Katrin's story was told in detail, using vivid descriptions from Annie, from Jaswanti, from Katrin's journal which had been lent to him, and from Katrin's father, whom he traveled to Munich to meet on his way home from India.

CHAPTER 28

_____ ANNIE _____

B y the time Annie finally looked at her email, she had 1,837 posts. The vast majority were some variety of spam: ads from companies she had once ordered something from, political opinion websites she'd signed up for, or ordinary no-excuse-for-it spam. It took most of an hour to pluck out these weeds to get down to the messages she actually wanted to read.

This still left nearly a hundred she felt responsible for. She tried to decide on a method. Did she want to start at the bottom, and read things in chronological order? Or had enough time gone by that she should start at the top and just pick up where things had now got to? Down at the bottom among the early arrivals were a number of messages from Ted with subject lines like: "Our Marriage," "I'm sorry," and "Bank account." Then came another series more like, "READ THIS!" and then "Don't Bother." Finally, messages from Ted seemed to peter out, except for one from a week ago, labelled "Divorce." She opened that one. Its surprisingly neutral tone read: "Annie, Please see attached. Call me if you have any questions or happen to be in town." What she downloaded was a Petition for Dissolution of Marriage. She stared at it for all of twenty minutes, trying to understand the legal language, the nature of Ted's demands, what it would mean to grant him the house on the bay (painful), the flip-house (welcome to it), the entire contents of their 401K (not going to happen), their paid-off MasterCard account (why not?), and his last name (is he kidding?). Besides the 401K, they each had separate retirement benefits from their employers, and also social security, so that wasn't in dispute, nor was custody, since the kids were grown up. Even though she was the one who had left, the finality of this document put her into shock.

She decided she'd better read all his emails. He had gone through all the stages of rage, grief, blame, bargaining, and finally acceptance. "Maybe you're right," he was saying in the last one before the final one, "maybe we would have spent the last years of our lives making each other miserable." Could he have ever come to such acceptance if she had stayed within reach?

She began to work through nineteen emails from Jen, moving backwards from the present. The most recent one: "Mom, guess what? Dad's got a girlfriend! You won't believe it! She's half his age. She's a realtor, the one who sold him that awful house. They are like swoony teenagers, hanging on each other and kissing all the time! It's embarrassing, but kinda cute. Do you mind? He seems really happy now, and I'm glad, because I couldn't take his crying all the time."

This was too many shocks for one day. Annie closed her laptop and went for a walk.

☆ ☆ ☆

Her walk turned into a hike northward along the gravel road on the eastern bank of the river. There were high bends and steep tracks off the main one down to the remoter ashrams clinging to the hillside. The sky was filled with puffy clouds that were not likely to rain, and the air felt clean and cool this high and this near the river. Once again, she felt free as the wind, but this time she analyzed the emotion with suspicion.

Did she really not care that her husband of thirty years was seeking a divorce, and was going to bring a new wife into her house on the bay? She thought hard about that. Wasn't she jealous? Maybe he had wanted a younger wife all along; didn't she care about that? Maybe his rude conduct toward her had always been his way of wanting freedom, but he was too bound by morals to acknowledge that even to himself. Then she thought how even her phrasing – 'too bound by morals' – stacked the case against him. Why not just say, he was too responsible to leave? Too morally disciplined? And that his deep-lying discontent had escaped through the bad humor he had been in most of his life.

Did that make a difference, putting it like that?

She tried a thought experiment. What if I go back, re-claim my house by the bay, mend things with Ted, have the kids over for a barbecue. Tell the stories of India as if she had just been on vacation. She realized she hadn't taken a single photo. That was strange; why not?

With a whirlwind of spinning gravel, a jeep came roaring past. Forest service officers gave a friendly wave before disappearing around the bend.

She hadn't brought a camera except for the one on her iPhone, which had died almost immediately. She could have gotten one if it had occurred to her to take photos. But weren't photos about a continuous life somewhere else? They were an attempt to hold two realities together. But she had brought no photos with her from her old life, and had taken none to take back with her. Her new life was a straight line, not a circle back again to the starting point.

No, she thought. I don't care. Let him have the house, the new wife, his own chance at starting over without a court fight and lawyer fees. He could keep the not-liquid equity in the house, and she would take the maximally liquid half of their 401k. She could probably get more, with a fight, but for her that was a fair enough trade. After that, she didn't ever want to think about it again.

She had sat down on a concrete milepost far north of town. The hillsides were steep here, and the river below in shadow. Above circled a hawk, not a vulture as she had first thought. Vultures had died out in India in the last decade, victims to liver failure caused by a medicine fed to the cows that were their main livelihood. You have to be able to change, Annie thought. You have to adapt to this earth and its lifeways. If you are being slowly poisoned by one way of life, you have to make a change. The vultures couldn't know that, but Annie did.

✫   ✫   ✫

She went back to work on the emails. She wrote a long account of recent events to Karen, who would be maximally interested in every detail, since she already knew almost all the players in the story. When she reached the end, the return of the stone to Shobha, she wrote:

"You know, a thought keeps occurring to me. That stone, found in a field, looked like it might have been hacked off a man-made image long ago. And, here's the strange part, there was a Kali image at the ashram that was really quite beautiful, that was missing its heel! But of course it's impossible that the heel, found in a field in Dehra Dun, could have come from an image that we know only recently was brought here from Kamakhya, and has now been taken back. That's all the way across North India. Impossible, right? Well, anyway, it's too late now to check. And Swamiji had both in his possession, and surely he would have picked up on it, if they had matched. Oh well."

Karen wrote back: "In India, anything is possible."

Annie stayed on contentedly, as the monsoons dwindled and died out, a period of beautiful fall came and went, replaced by seriously cold weather that crept down from the north with thick mists that filled the valley and hid the river from sight. She wrapped herself in blankets on Lonnie's patio, and continued to work over her computer books and her laptop. She started a blog devoted to the stories of the women she had met in Rishikesh. And before long – before Christmas – she began to think of going someplace else.

Made in the USA
Lexington, KY
02 April 2012